MARE IN THE MEADOW

'Rhian, this is Mandy Hope,' her mother said encouragingly. 'She and her friend have been riding the horse in Mrs Tandy's field.'

'I thought maybe you'd like to come and say hello to her,' Mandy offered. 'And you could come with us when we take her out, if you want.'

'What do you think, Rhian?' Mrs Jones said, smiling hopefully at her daughter. 'That sounds like fun, doesn't it? Wouldn't you like to go with them?'

Rhian shot Mandy a long, cool look. 'I can't come, right now,' she said abruptly. 'I'm a bit busy at the moment. Sorry.'

'Oh, go on – why not, love?' her mother said. 'You used to be so interested in horses!'

'Yes, I *used* to be,' Rhian said deliberately. 'But I'm not any more, OK? I wish you'd just accept the fact! Give it a rest will you?' And with that she turned and stomped back up the stairs.

Animal Ark series

Plus:
Little Animal Ark
Animal Ark Pets
Animal Ark Hauntings
Animal Ark Holiday Specials

LUCY DANIELS

Mare
— in the —
Meadow

Illustrations by Ann Baum

**Hodder
Children's
Books**

a division of Hodder Headline Limited

Special thanks to Jennie Walters
Thanks also to C. J. Hall, B.Vet.Med., M.R.C.V.S., for reviewing
the veterinary information contained in this book.

Animal Ark is a trademark of Working Partners Limited
Text copyright © 2001 Working Partners Limited
Created by Working Partners Limited, London W6 0QT
Original series created by Ben M. Baglio
Illustrations copyright © 2001 Ann Baum

First published in Great Britain in 2001
by Hodder Children's Books

For more information about Animal Ark,
please contact www.animalark.co.uk

8

A Catalogue record for this book is available from the British Library

ISBN 0 340 77883 0

Typeset by Avon DataSet Ltd, Bidford-on-Avon, Warwickshire

Printed and bound in Great Britain by
Clays Ltd, St Ives plc

The paper and board used in this paperback by
Hodder Children's Books are natural recyclable products
made from wood grown in sustainable forests.
The manufacturing processes conform to the environmental
regulations of the country of origin.

Hodder Children's Books
a division of Hodder Headline Limited
338 Euston Road
London NW1 3BH

One

'Oh, Smoky!' Mandy Hope smiled, stroking the grey cat's soft tummy. 'I think you must be the cutest thing in the world!'

Smoky was lying on his back on her grandparents' sofa, his tail curled up neatly over his stomach and his front paws crossed across his chest. He closed his eyes and turned his head to one side with what looked like a very satisfied expression. Mandy tickled him behind the ear, before turning back to the photos her grandfather was passing over from his chair next to her.

'There's another shot of your gran in front of

Lake Windermere,' he said. 'And look – here we are together, in the very same spot! A Japanese lady kindly took that one for us.'

'Lovely,' Mandy said politely, adding the pictures to the growing pile on her lap. 'You must have had a great time.'

Her grandparents had just come back from a late-summer break in the Lake District, and Mandy had dropped in after school on Friday to hear all about it. She was doing her best to concentrate on their holiday snaps, but delicious smells were wafting through from the kitchen, and she was longing to sample the jam tarts she'd just spotted her gran taking out of the oven. Dorothy Hope was in charge of refreshments for the Women's Institute monthly talk the next evening, and the little kitchen at Lilac Cottage was already crowded with cakes, scones and pastries. Surely there'd be one or two to spare . . . ?

Her grandfather was unstoppable, though. 'Oh, it was a grand holiday!' he continued enthusiastically, handing over another couple of pictures. 'Look at the colour of the sky in this photo! It's Windermere again, round the other side of the lake. And not a cloud to be seen! That's what's so good about our camper van – we can just take off if the weather's fine.'

'And how did Smoky feel about Mrs Jackson coming in to feed him?' Mandy asked, stroking the cat's tummy again. 'You know I wouldn't have minded helping out.'

'Well, we didn't want to bother you, what with the new term starting,' her grandfather replied. 'Rhona was watering the garden for us anyway, so she was happy to look after Smoky too.' Then a frown crossed his face. 'Mind you, she said he didn't seem to eat much. Hardly touched his food towards the end of the week.'

'Perhaps he was missing you,' Mandy suggested, tidying up the sheaf of photos after her grandfather had handed over the last ones. She put them all away in the wallet, trying not to show her relief.

Tom Hope shook his head. 'I don't think so. You know what cats are like – more attached to places than people. As long as Smoky's on his home patch, he's usually fine. Besides, he's still off his food.'

Mandy glanced anxiously at the young cat. Smoky's mother had been a starving stray, so

Mandy and her best friend, James Hunter, had helped rear the four kittens in her litter and find them homes. She'd first seen Smoky when he was only a few hours old, and she was the one who'd persuaded her grandparents to take him in. She knew her gran and grandad doted on Smoky, but she still felt responsible for him in a funny kind of way. Gently, she lifted him on to her lap for a closer examination.

'Hmm, perhaps he is a little thinner,' she said, looking at Smoky's ribcage. And then she noticed something even more worrying. 'Look, Grandad,' she said, putting a hand under Smoky's chin and raising his head. 'Is that a lump on his face, just under his eye? Or am I imagining things?'

'Oh, no, love, I don't think you are,' said Tom Hope, peering anxiously at Smoky's face. 'It certainly does look swollen round there.'

'And he's dribbling a bit, too,' Mandy said, feeling some saliva trickle on to her fingers and wiping them on her school skirt. It was already flecked with paint from that afternoon's art class and due for a wash. 'I think we should take him along to Animal Ark, don't you?' she asked her grandfather. 'Mum or Dad can take a look at him, just to be on the safe side. They're not that busy at the moment.'

Mandy's parents, Adam and Emily Hope, were both vets. They ran a surgery on the other side of Welford, and Mandy loved helping them look after their patients. She thought that nursing a sick animal back to health and sending it home, on the road to recovery, was the most rewarding thing in the world. Sometimes there was heartache, too – when a much-loved pet didn't respond to treatment or had to be put to sleep – but that didn't stop her from wanting to be a vet herself when she was older.

'Well, I've made enough food for an army, let alone Welford WI!' exclaimed Dorothy Hope, drying her hands on a tea towel as she came into the sitting-room. 'What would you like to try, love?'

Mandy wasn't feeling so hungry any more. 'We think Smoky might need a check-up at Animal Ark, Gran,' she said, jumping to her feet. 'His face looks rather swollen, and that might be why he's off his food.'

'Do you really think so?' said her grandmother, putting down the towel and becoming instantly practical. 'Oh, poor Smoky! I'll get his carrying cage from the basement.' She turned to her husband, who was standing there wringing his hands and looking miserably at the cat. 'It's not far, but we might as well drive him over – don't you think, Tom? That cage is awkward to carry any distance.'

'Yes, you're right,' he said, feeling in his trouser pockets for the keys. 'I'll get the car out right away.' And with one last glance at Smoky, he hurried out of the room.

Mandy and her gran smiled at each other. They both knew how soft-hearted Tom Hope was – he couldn't even bear to watch when Smoky had his vaccinations. Mandy could see Gran's eyes were troubled, though, and there was a chill in the pit of her own stomach. What if there was something seriously wrong with Smoky, like a tumour or some other kind of horrible growth under his skin?

'Better not waste any time,' said her gran, heading for the basement.

Mandy picked Smoky up tenderly and cuddled him against her chest, burying her face for a moment in his silky fur. 'Don't worry, Smoky,' she whispered. 'We'll soon sort you out.' But she

didn't feel quite as confident as she sounded.

'What do you think it could be, Dad?' Mandy asked, when she couldn't bear the suspense any longer. Simon, the practice nurse, was holding Smoky securely on the table in one of the treatment rooms at Animal Ark, while Adam Hope studied the inside of his mouth. Mandy and her grandparents were clustered anxiously round them.

'I'm pretty sure he's got an abscess at the root of one of his top teeth,' her father answered, as

Smoky began to struggle in Simon's grip. He'd been very patient so far, but now he seemed to have decided enough was enough.

'There's a good boy, Smoky,' Mr Hope went on, releasing the cat's jaws and giving him a soothing stroke. 'We're all done for the moment.'

'And it's making his face swell?' Mandy asked, holding open the lid of the carrying cage so Simon could pop Smoky back inside.

'Probably,' said her father, peeling off the thin plastic gloves he was wearing. 'The tooth that I think is infected has roots which end in the bone under Smoky's eye, and the abscess will be full of fluid. We'll take an X-ray, just to make sure. If my diagnosis is correct, the tooth will have to come out so that the abscess can drain.'

'But then he'll be all right?' Mandy said, taking a quick look at her grandfather's worried face.

'I'm sure he will be,' said Mr Hope reassuringly. 'We'll take a blood test too, just to be on the safe side. And we can even give his teeth a going over with our wonderful new ultrasonic descaler.' He put his arm round his father's shoulders and added, 'Don't worry, Dad. We'll give Smoky the five-star treatment, and he'll be back playing football with you in the garden before you know it!'

That made everyone laugh, and some of the tension in the room seemed to melt away.

'There you are, Dorothy,' Tom Hope said gruffly, patting his wife on the back. 'I told you having a vet for a son would come in handy one day.'

'Well, what a relief,' she said thankfully. 'I've been feeling so awful that we hadn't noticed anything before. It's been such a rush, coming back from holiday and trying to catch up with everything. Anyway, what happens now? Do we leave him here with you?'

'We'll need to keep him in overnight.' It was Simon who answered the question, as he fastened Smoky's carrying cage securely. 'When was the last time he had something to eat?'

'Oh, he hasn't eaten all day,' Mandy's gran replied quickly.

'That's just as well,' Simon said with a smile. 'Then we should be able to take the X-ray straight away and whip that tooth out today. You'll probably be able to come and fetch him tomorrow.'

Smoky peered out at them and gave a mournful miaow. 'Don't worry,' Mandy whispered, tickling him under the chin through the bars of the cage. 'You're in very good hands.'

Both Mandy's parents were wonderful vets and, as they often said, Simon was one of the best practice nurses you could hope to find. He might look young, with his spiky blond hair and wire-rimmed glasses, but he was very efficient – and caring, too. He had a gentle way of handling frightened animals that always helped to calm them down.

There was still a final suspicion nagging away in the back of Mandy's mind, though. 'Dad,' she began, after her grandparents had left and Simon had taken Smoky through to the operating room, 'if you think Smoky has an abscess, why do you need to take a blood test?'

'I just want to make sure that he's in good health generally,' her father replied, already busy wiping down the table with disinfectant spray.

'But why shouldn't he be?' Mandy persisted. 'Surely the only reason he's thin is because he hasn't been eating properly?'

'Yes, I'm almost certain that's it,' Mr Hope said,

scratching his dark beard and frowning. 'But if a cat's having mouth problems, there's a very slight chance that his immune system might not be working properly. We need to check there are no kidney problems or signs of feline leukaemia, for example. Young cats can be prone to that.'

'Oh no!' Mandy gasped. 'You don't really think—'

Mr Hope cut across her words. 'Now, look, I don't want you getting worried,' he said firmly, guiding her out of the room and towards the interconnecting door that led through to their old stone cottage. 'Smoky's had all his jabs and it's very unlikely there's an underlying infection. But I wouldn't be doing my job if I didn't cover every possibility, would I?'

'I suppose not,' Mandy said, trying not to read too much into her father's words. Still, she couldn't help feeling concerned. Smoky was one of the family, and there was no way her mind would be at rest until he'd been given the all-clear.

'Can I help you with the X-ray?' she asked next. Keeping busy might stop her imagining the worst.

'No thanks, love. Simon and I can manage,' her father replied as he ushered her out of the surgery. 'I think Mum's back from her rounds, so why don't you see if she needs a hand with supper? I'll let you know how everything's gone the minute we're finished, I promise.'

And Mandy had to be content with that.

Emily Hope's green eyes were thoughtful as she sipped her tea and listened to Mandy explain about Smoky.

'I can't help worrying that something might be seriously wrong,' she finished by saying. 'What do *you* think, Mum?'

'I think your father's quite right, love,' Mrs Hope replied. 'There don't seem to be any other signs of kidney problems and there's only a tiny chance of leukaemia, particularly as Smoky's had all his jabs. Anyway, there's certainly no point in you fretting about it. That won't help, will it?'

'No, I guess not,' Mandy admitted, shrugging her shoulders.

Mrs Hope smiled and reached across the table to squeeze her hand. 'I know how much you care about Smoky,' she said, 'but you know Dad and Simon will look after him. Try not to upset yourself, love. Think about something else for a change. Or why don't you get out of the house and go for a walk? It's still a lovely day.'

'Maybe,' Mandy said, getting up from the table and stretching her arms over her head. 'I could give James a ring.'

'Might as well make the most of this slack time. Things are going to be quite hectic round here very soon,' her mother warned. 'You know that Simon's going away tomorrow?'

'Of course!' Mandy replied. She'd forgotten about Simon taking three weeks' holiday in South Africa to visit a college friend of his who was living out there now. 'Oh, I'm glad he was here to help look after Smoky! What are we going to do while he's away, Mum?'

'I've managed to find a nursing student who needs some work experience,' Emily Hope replied, pouring herself another mug of tea. 'She hasn't quite finished her training, but she seems very keen and eager to learn. I'm sure we'll be able to cope between us.'

'I should think so,' Mandy said. 'After all, I can help her in the surgery to begin with, if I'm around – tell her where things are, that kind of thing.'

'Just so long as you remember the rule,' Mrs Hope said, gathering her long auburn hair into a ponytail and shooting Mandy a look from under her eyebrows. 'Schoolwork first, animals later. It's the start of a new school year and you're going to have to study hard.'

'I know, Mum,' Mandy said. She'd heard the rule so many times she could repeat it in her sleep. And then, through the window she suddenly spotted a couple of familiar figures coming down the path.

'Oh look, here are James and Blackie,' she said, cheering up straight away. She couldn't help feeling happier at the sight of the excited Labrador winding his lead into knots round James's legs. 'Perhaps that walk would be a good idea.'

'I'm going to take Blackie for a training session on the green,' James said, after Mandy had opened the front door. 'He's beginning to get very naughty again. D'you want to come?'

'Great!' Mandy replied, grabbing a sweatshirt. If she couldn't help with Smoky, she'd sooner not be in the house at all. 'See you in an hour or so, Mum,' she called, setting off with James.

As they walked down the lane, she began telling Smoky's story all over again. James was very concerned about the cat too. When Smoky was a tiny kitten, James had bottle-fed him plenty of times, so he knew him well. Besides, he'd also given a home to another of the kittens in the litter: Smoky's brother, whom he'd called Eric.

'Smoky's so young, though!' he said worriedly. 'It was awful when we discovered Benji had a brain tumour, but at least he'd had a good life.'

'Oh, don't!' Mandy groaned, remembering how sad James had been when his old cat, the one before Eric, had been put to sleep. Now it was her turn to try to reassure James, and herself at the same time. 'Smoky can't have leukaemia,' she said firmly. 'He's had his jabs, so it's very unlikely. I'm sure Dad's right – it's only an abscess.'

Mandy forced herself to concentrate on dog training, rather than worrying about Smoky. Blackie was pulling a lot on the lead so they had to keep stopping, to try and make him walk properly to heel. And then just when the labrador was beginning to behave himself, he spotted a cat sunning itself on a low stone wall and decided it was time to play.

'Tell Blackie he'll be off to Mrs Ponsonby's if he doesn't toe the line,' Mandy joked, as James was dragged down the lane behind the panting, eager Labrador. Mrs Ponsonby was a very bossy woman who lived in the village with her two dogs – a pedigree Pekinese called Pandora and a mongrel, Toby. She'd once organised dog obedience classes, but they hadn't worked for Blackie.

It was a sunny, early September evening and several people were out in their front gardens. Mandy said hello to all of them and waved across the street to Mrs McFarlane, who was closing the post office for the evening. Mandy had lived in Welford all her life, ever since Emily and Adam Hope had adopted her as a baby after her birth parents were killed in a car crash. She knew pretty well everyone in the village, and their pets too. Through an upstairs window of the Fox and Goose, she could see the dark head of John Hardy, whose father ran the pub. John had two rabbits – Button and Barney. The big ginger tom that Blackie was trying to play with was one of Walter Pickard's three cats; they lived in one of the cottages that were in a row behind the Fox and

Goose. Walter's neighbour Ernie Bell had a pet squirrel, Sammy, and a tortoiseshell cat called Amy, who was Smoky and Eric's sister.

Despite her good intentions, thoughts of Smoky suddenly came flooding back into Mandy's mind. Her father should be taking out his tooth around now, and testing a blood sample too. *Oh, please let everything be OK!* she thought to herself. And she crossed her fingers so tightly that they hurt.

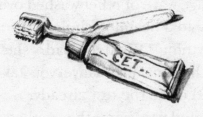

Two

A little while later, Mandy was setting the table for supper. She'd said goodbye to James and Blackie on the village green after an hour or so, and hurried back to Animal Ark to see if there was any news about Smoky. There had been no sign of her father, though. Surely he should have finished the operation by now? What was taking him so long? One of her mother's cheese and pasta bakes was bubbling away in the oven, but Mandy still couldn't summon up much of an appetite.

All of a sudden, Adam Hope put his head round

the kitchen door. Mandy held her breath as she searched his face for a sign of how things had gone. A huge wave of relief washed over her when he broke into a beaming smile.

'Is everything OK then, Dad?' she asked, her own face lighting up. 'Have you taken out the tooth? And done the test already?'

'Yes, yes and yes,' her father replied. 'The tooth came out all in one piece and I'm sure the abscess will heal up quickly. And we ran the tests for kidney disease and leukaemia ourselves just now. Smoky's absolutely fine – no sign of any problems at all.'

'Oh, that's great!' Mandy said, letting the knives and forks crash in a heap on the scrubbed pine table and hurrying over to give her father a hug. 'Have you told Gran and Grandad? They'll be so pleased!'

'I'm going to ring them right away.' Mr Hope smiled, disentangling himself. 'Is Mum around?'

'Doing some yoga in the living-room,' Mandy answered. 'I'll go and tell her the good news. And then can I see Smoky, Dad?'

'Sure,' he replied, already making his way to the phone in the hall. 'Simon's just settling him into the residential unit. I think it's best if we keep an eye on him tonight, but he should be able to go home in the morning.'

Mandy looked into the living-room. Her mother was standing on one leg, the other making a triangular shape against it, with her arms raised in a circle above her head.

'Pretending to be a tree, Mum?' Mandy grinned cheekily. She felt as though the cares of the world had been lifted off her shoulders. 'Thought I'd let you know that Dad says Smoky's going to be fine.'

'That's wonderful news, love!' Mrs Hope said with a broad smile, carefully lowering her leg. 'Gran and Grandad will be delighted. And by the way, this pose *is* called The Tree.' She raised her leg again before adding solemnly, 'It's very good for your balance. Supper in ten minutes, OK?'

'Great!' Mandy called over her shoulder. Suddenly, she felt starving.

She arrived at the residential unit to find Simon lowering a very dozy-looking Smoky into a basket in one of the pens. His golden eyes were only half open and immediately he curled up to sleep in the basket.

'How is he?' she asked quietly, going over to take a look.

'Well, he came round from the anaesthetic very nicely,' Simon said, shutting the cage door. 'We gave him as light a dose as we possibly could, and he's been under the infrared lamp for a while.'

'Oh yes, to keep his body temperature up,' Mandy said. She knew how important it was for animals to stay warm when they were recovering from the effects of an anaesthetic.

'That's right,' Simon nodded. 'I bet he'll soon be feeling a lot better than he has for some time. That tooth must have been giving him a lot of trouble.'

'Poor Smoky,' Mandy said, giving the cat a sympathetic smile. His eyes twitched open briefly at the sound of her voice, but closed again as soon as he had shifted into a more comfortable position.

'Well, I'll have to leave Smoky in your tender care. It's about time I was going,' Simon said, after he'd filled up a water bowl and put it in the young cat's pen. 'I haven't even started packing yet!'

'Are you excited?' Mandy asked, a little enviously. She'd had a wonderful working holiday with James and her parents in South Africa, seeing all kinds of amazing animals. She knew Simon was in for a treat.

'You bet!' he replied, taking off his white coat and rolling it into a bundle which he stuck under his arm. 'Jim rang a couple of days ago to tell me he's fixed up a whale-watching expendition at the Cape, and we're going to spend a few days in a game reserve, too.' He gazed at Smoky and added thoughtfully, 'I wonder what it's like taking out a lion's tooth? Much the same, I suppose.'

'Don't stay away too long,' Mandy teased. 'We'll miss you.' She knew how much her parents relied on Simon's quiet, efficient help in the surgery.

'I'll be back before you know it,' Simon said, opening the door of the unit and standing aside to let Mandy go through first. 'Anyway, I'm sure everything will be fine. You're in charge – OK?'

'OK,' Mandy grinned, clapping the hand he was holding up in a high five. Then they turned off the light and left Smoky alone in the dark, quiet room.

'Here he is,' Mandy said proudly, lifting Smoky out of his cage the next morning. 'He ate a good

breakfast and now he's as right as rain.' She passed the cat over to her grandfather, who was beaming from ear to ear.

'He certainly looks in good shape,' Tom Hope said, scratching behind Smoky's ears and making him purr loudly. 'It must be a dose of your TLC that's done the trick, Mandy.'

'Well, I think it was Dad and Simon taking his tooth out, rather than my tender loving care this time,' Mandy said and smiled.

'Thank you so much for helping to look after

him, dear,' said Mandy's gran, putting an arm round her shoulders. 'We're really delighted everything turned out so well.'

Adam Hope came through from the surgery, waving a toothbrush in the air. 'Found my samples at last!' he said. 'If you can get in the habit of brushing Smoky's teeth fairly regularly with this, it'll help keep them in good condition.'

'You can rub his teeth with some tuna water at first, to get him used to the feeling,' Mandy advised. 'That helps, doesn't it, Dad?'

'Certainly does,' Mr Hope said. 'But lots of cats love the taste of toothpaste, so you might find Smoky thinks having his teeth brushed is a treat.'

Tom Hope loaded Smoky carefully into the carrying cage and latched it at the top. 'Time to get this fellow home for some more spoiling,' he said, as Smoky miaowed pitifully from inside. 'He's got quite a few meals to catch up on, I reckon.'

'You know, a lump of raw meat once a week is good for teeth cleaning too,' Mandy's father added. 'All that gristle and connective tissue acts like dental floss for animals.'

'Dad!' Mandy pulled a face. She was a

vegetarian, which made the thought of eating gristle and tissue even more disgusting.

Her gran didn't bat an eyelid, though. 'There's a piece of stewing steak in the fridge,' she said. 'We could give him some this evening. Oh, I hope the WI talk doesn't go on too long! I could do with an early night after all this worry.'

'Shall I come and help?' Mandy suggested. 'It's the weekend, and I don't have much homework. I could see if James is free, too.'

'Would you mind, love?' her grandmother said. 'It would be wonderful if you could give us a hand. Mrs Ponsonby was going to be serving refreshments with me but she's in bed with flu. Mind you, I don't think James will want to come. Wild-flower conservation might not be quite his thing.'

'I'll see what I can do to persuade him,' Mandy said. The evening would be much more fun if James was there too, and it would be good to have some extra help. 'Don't worry – I'll think of something to get him along!'

'Well, I'd say that was a great success,' Dorothy Hope declared, beginning to stack the chairs after the talk was over that evening and nearly everyone had left. 'And thanks for your help, you two. I'd never have managed without you.'

'That's OK,' Mandy said, giving her a hand. 'It was quite interesting, really. I had no idea how many different flowers you could find in one field. And the photos were great, weren't they, James?'

James was looking round the village hall, his arms folded and a doubtful expression on his face. 'Just look at all the mess!' he said, shaking his head. 'It's going to take us ages to clear this lot up.'

The tables were littered with dirty crockery, glasses and cutlery. All that remained of the mountain of cakes and pastries in the kitchen were platefuls of crumbs, a couple of broken jam tarts and a slice of cherry cake that someone had dropped on the floor and then trodden on.

'Do you need any help?' said a friendly voice, and they turned round to see a pleasant-looking woman hovering nearby. She was short and slight, with curly grey hair, round blue eyes and arched eyebrows that gave her a surprised expression.

'Well, that's very kind of you,' Dorothy Hope began. 'Are you sure you wouldn't mind? There is a fair amount of work to be done.'

'Not at all,' said the woman warmly, beginning to roll up her sleeves. 'I love tidying up and putting things in order. Just show me where everything is and I'll get started right away. If you can bring me the plates and cups, I'll wash them up.'

'Do you live round here?' James asked, once he and Mandy had shown their new volunteer through to the kitchen.

'I don't think we've seen you in Welford before,' Mandy added.

'Oh, of course – I should have introduced myself,' the woman said, putting a hand on Mandy's arm. 'I'm Mrs Tandy, Eleanor Tandy. I live some way out of the village, and this is the first WI talk I've been to, so that's why we don't know each other. I just *had* to come tonight. Once I heard that a botanist was coming to talk about wild flowers, I said to myself, "Eleanor, that is one talk you simply mustn't miss." '

'Oh,' said Mandy, rather bemused by this flood of information. 'Well, I'm Mandy Hope and this is my friend James Hunter. My gran is the chairwoman of Welford WI – she made all the cakes tonight.'

'She's certainly a very good cook,' said Mrs Tandy, running a sinkful of hot water and squirting in some washing-up liquid. 'But it was learning about wild flowers that really drew me here tonight. There's a meadow behind my house, you see, and it's absolutely full of them.' She turned round to gaze at James and Mandy worriedly. 'That's the trouble. What if Camomile's been eating some rare plant that I don't know about? I'm going to have a good look round that meadow first thing tomorrow morning and see exactly what's in it.' She frowned and started collecting up some of the dirty cups and saucers that were dotted round the kitchen.

James and Mandy looked at each other, perplexed. Mandy shrugged her shoulders, to show James she had no more idea what Mrs Tandy was talking about than he had. 'Who's Camomile?' she asked.

But Mrs Tandy had plunged her hands into the soapy water and was starting to wash up at a furious pace. 'Now that's enough chitchat,' she said. 'Let's see how quickly we can get things clean and tidy.'

As she and James dried the clean crockery,

Mandy found herself wondering about Camomile. Who – or what – could she be? When everything had been packed away in the cupboard at last and Miss Davy had finished stacking all the chairs, she thought it was safe to ask Mrs Tandy again.

'Camomile belongs to my daughter,' Mrs Tandy began, letting the washing-up water drain out of the sink. 'But Laura's just gone off to America, so she's left Camomile with me. I keep her in the field behind my house. Such a responsibility! She's a lovely creature, of course, and she makes such a pretty picture there in the meadow, but I do worry about her.'

'Yes, but what *is* she?' James asked, when he could get a word in edgeways. 'What kind of animal?'

'Oh, how silly of me!' Mrs Tandy exclaimed, drying her hands on a tea towel. 'She's a pony. Well, a horse, really – or a mare, to be strictly accurate. A palomino mare, with a beautiful golden coat and a cream mane and tail.'

Mandy was immediately interested. A mare in the meadow – it sounded lovely!

'Do you two know anything about horses?' Mrs

Tandy asked James and Mandy.

'Yes, quite a bit,' Mandy answered for both of them. 'Neither of us have a horse, but we know how to ride. And my parents are both vets, so I've learned a lot from them. Why? Do you need a hand with Camomile?'

Mrs Tandy sighed and laid down the towel. 'Well, I'm not quite sure what to do at the moment,' she said. 'Laura used to keep a pony in the field when she was younger, so I know how to look after Camomile – feed her and take care of her health, that sort of thing – but I'm too old to start riding her. She's quite a size. I shouldn't think I could even get up in the saddle!'

'Your daughter doesn't expect you to, though, does she?' James asked, looking slightly startled.

'Oh no,' Mrs Tandy said, smiling at the very idea. 'It was all arranged that a friend of hers would come to exercise Camomile three or four times a week. She was meant to start yesterday, after Camomile had settled in with me, but there was no sign of her all morning. When I rang to find out where she was, her mother told me she'd had the chance to work at a pony-trekking centre in Scotland. So she'd gone off the night before, without so much as a by-your-leave!'

'And you've been left in the lurch. Or rather, Camomile has,' Mandy said. No wonder Mrs Tandy was looking worried.

'I don't know what to do,' she confessed, leaning against the sink. 'I could advertise for someone to come and ride her, but I don't really want a complete stranger turning up. What would Laura say if I let Camomile go off with someone who couldn't ride her properly?'

'Have you talked to Laura about it?' James asked. 'Perhaps she could suggest someone else.'

Mrs Tandy shook her head. 'Laura doesn't have a phone yet. She's only been in America a couple of days, and I can't contact her till she rings me.' She sighed again, and then looked appealingly at James and Mandy. 'I don't suppose you two have any spare time on your hands, by any chance? I feel as though I could trust you, though I know we've only just met.'

'I should think so,' Mandy answered quickly, looking into Mrs Tandy's anxious eyes. The two of them were just about the same height. 'James and I would love to help you exercise Camomile. Maybe not three or four times a week, but we could come over at the weekend, couldn't we, James? It would be a pleasure!'

Three

'I'm not so sure about this, Mandy,' James said, as they waited for Dorothy Hope to lock up the village hall and give them a lift home. 'We're not really going to solve all Mrs Tandy's problems at all, are we? There's no way we can get out there to exercise her horse in the week, and the odd ride at weekends won't be enough.'

'No, you're right,' Mandy admitted. Perhaps she hadn't really thought the whole thing through. 'I'd love to meet Camomile, though, wouldn't you? And maybe we could think of someone else who might be able to exercise her, once we've got to know her a little.'

She felt in her pocket for the scrap of paper Mrs Tandy had given her before she left, with her phone number scribbled on. 'It wouldn't do any harm to go along tomorrow, at least,' she said to James. 'I just need to check with Mum and Dad first, and see what Gran knows about Mrs Tandy.'

'I shouldn't think she's a mad axe murderer,' James said with a smile. 'She might end up talking us to death, though.'

It turned out that Gran knew Mrs Tandy's next-door neighbour, who confirmed that she was just as respectable as she seemed to be. And Emily Hope was quite happy to drive Mandy and James out to see her the next day, so the visit was arranged for that Sunday afternoon.

'After all,' Mandy said to James in the car on Sunday, 'even if we only take Camomile out for a ride today, that'll still be a help, won't it?' She fiddled with the drawstring at the bottom of her fleece and added eagerly, 'How much further is it, Mum?'

'Nearly there,' Emily Hope smiled. 'As long as we don't get lost, that is.'

Mandy couldn't wait to see Camomile. From what Mrs Tandy had said, the mare sounded lovely – very sweet-tempered and gentle. It would be wonderful to saddle her up and go off for a good long ride.

They managed to find Mrs Tandy's house very easily. It was a neat-looking bungalow on the outskirts of the nearby town of Walton. As Mandy had expected, the place was immaculately clean and tidy inside, too.

'What a wonderful view!' Emily Hope exclaimed as Mrs Tandy showed them through into her sitting-room. Every surface gleamed, and the air smelled of lavender furniture polish. Sparkling French windows looked out on to a small garden and, beyond that, a lush green field with a wooden fence around it.

'So that's your wild-flower meadow,' James said, walking up to the window for a closer look. 'Are there any rare plants in it, do you think?'

'Well, it's quite difficult to tell,' Mrs Tandy said, hovering behind him. 'Most of them have stopped flowering now, of course. But this morning I *think* I found a clump of fragrant orchids growing near the garden gate. Camomile seems to have left them alone, thank goodness.'

'And where is Camomile?' Mandy asked, craning her head to look. 'Can we go and see her straight away?'

'Mandy!' Mrs Hope frowned, but Mrs Tandy was already opening the French windows and didn't seem at all put out by her impatience.

'Of course,' she said with a smile. 'Here, take these peppermints and she'll be your friend for life.'

They all walked through the garden and down to the field. 'My late husband was a builder,' Mrs Tandy explained. 'He bought this plot of land and put up all the houses along this stretch of the road. We kept the meadow for Laura's pony, and even after we sold him, we liked the view so much that we kept it as it was.'

'Good for you!' Mandy said, looking over the gate. 'It's lovely to have some green space in the middle of all these houses.'

'And it's good grazing, too,' Mrs Hope added. 'Plenty of meadow grass and some clover, too.' She bent down and examined a plant with pretty blue flowers. 'This is wild chicory, I think,' she said, breaking off a stem to show Mrs Tandy. 'It has lots of minerals in it – excellent for horses.'

The meadow was more of a large paddock, really, with a tall oak tree in the middle. A second gate opened out on to the road, and there was a stable in one corner with a water trough next to it.

'And this must be Camomile. Oh, she's gorgeous!' Mandy breathed, as a beautiful palomino mare came trotting towards them from the far edge of the field. She held her head proudly and her long silky mane rippled in the breeze. Powerful muscles bunched and flowed under her golden coat as she moved with a smooth, easy grace.

Mandy handed James a couple of peppermints and held out one herself, flat on the palm of her hand so Camomile could take it easily. The horse's whiskery lips twitched as she delicately picked up the mint, brushing against Mandy's skin and making her smile. James reached forward to rub Camomile's nose. She snickered a couple of times, pushing her muzzle against his hand.

'I think you've found her favourite spot,' Emily Hope commented, patting Camomile's shoulder.

Mrs Tandy looked on proudly. 'You can see,

despite her size, that she's just a big softie,' she said. 'Gentle as a lamb, she is, and Laura's always telling me a three-year-old child could ride her. Now what's the word she uses? Bomb-proof, that's it.'

She started to open the gate, adding, 'Come along with me and I'll show you where her saddle and bridle are. Then I'll leave you to it and take your mother inside for a cup of tea.'

'You can go first,' James whispered to Mandy as they walked behind Mrs Tandy across the field to the stable. 'Camomile's a bit bigger than I was expecting.'

'But bigger horses are often the easiest to ride,' Mandy whispered back. 'They don't twist and turn quite so much. And just look at the way she's following us. She's an angel!'

Mandy felt sure she could detect an eager look in the mare's eye, as though she was looking forward to the ride too. 'Where should we take her?' she asked Mrs Tandy.

'Well, if you go out of the far gate on to the road and turn right into Green Lane, you'll eventually come to a bridle-path on the left, after all the houses have petered out,' she replied. 'It goes in a circle, round the edge of the wood, so you can't get lost.'

Mrs Tandy took James and Mandy into the stable to show them where everything was, while Mrs Hope made friends with Camomile outside. The mare's tack was on the other side of a partition, together with a fleecy numnah – a cloth to go under the saddle – and a grooming kit in a plastic container: some brushes, sponges, cloths, rubber currycombs and a couple of hoof picks. There was also a headcollar with a rope attached to it. A hard hat that must have been Laura's stood on a shelf, but James and Mandy had brought their own.

'Great!' Mandy said, picking up the headcollar. 'We can tie Camomile to something and give her a quick brush over before we saddle her up. It looks like she's been rolling in the dirt.'

James took the grooming kit and they went back outside. Mrs Tandy showed them a ring on the stable wall where they could tether Camomile. With the help of a couple more peppermints, Mandy had soon slipped the headcollar over the mare's head and she was safely secured. James chose a body brush for himself, passed one over to Mandy, and began to tackle a patch of mud on the mare's flanks.

'You can tell she's got a lovely temperament,' Emily Hope said admiringly, stroking the horse's bowed neck. 'See how patiently she's standing!'

'And she's healthy too, isn't she, Mum?' Mandy asked.

'Looks like it,' Mrs Hope replied, running her hands down Camomile's foreleg. 'I checked her teeth just now and they're in good condition.' She picked up Camomile's leg and examined her hoof carefully before letting it rest back down on the ground.

'I'm just worried she's going to get bored on her own in this field all day,' Mrs Tandy said. 'Laura used to ride her most days after work, you see. She kept her at a stable, but she fed and mucked her out herself. There's no way we can afford to keep her at full livery while Laura's away, but I can't really manage her on my own.'

'We'll come as often as we can,' Mandy began, but then she caught James's warning look and bit her tongue. He was right – they lived too far away and were too busy with other commitments to be of much help. It would be a mistake to make Mrs

Tandy feel she could rely on them, and then let her down. She began to brush Camomile's coat with smooth, sweeping strokes. Well, they were here now. And at least for today they could give Camomile a thorough grooming, and as long a ride as she wanted. That would be a pleasure!

'Now, you're sure you'll be OK, love?' Mandy's mum asked her, as she and Mrs Tandy prepared to go back to the house.

'We'll be fine,' Mandy said confidently, giving the mare's mane a final comb. 'We'll take Camomile round the meadow first, just to get used to her – but you've seen how sweet and steady she is, haven't you?'

'Yes, you're right. Well, have a great time then,' said Mrs Hope, giving her a quick kiss goodbye. 'Mrs Tandy's going to drop you and James back when you've finished. Now, who's going first?'

'That'll be me,' Mandy said, leading Camomile over to the mounting block near the water trough that Mrs Tandy had pointed out earlier. She held the reins bunched loosely in her left hand, stuck her left foot in the stirrup and started hauling herself up on to Camomile's back while James pulled down on the opposite stirrup to stop the saddle slipping. Camomile stood quietly while Mandy got herself organised – tightening the girth and shortening the stirrups a couple of notches. Then she took up the reins, squeezed her heels against the mare's sides, and they were off!

Camomile was wonderfully smooth to ride, and Mandy found herself grinning broadly as they walked round the edge of the field at a brisk, collected pace. She shortened the reins a little, gave the lightest touch with her heels, and the mare immediately broke into the balanced, comfortable trot they had seen earlier. Mandy waved triumphantly, and her mother and Mrs Tandy waved back, before turning to leave the field.

'Good girl,' Mandy said, as she adjusted to the rhythm of Camomile's trot, patting her neck encouragingly. The mare's ears flicked back and forth and she whinnied and shook her blonde mane, as if to say that she was really enjoying herself too.

Mandy looked round to give James a thumbs-up when, all of a sudden, she caught sight of someone staring down at her and Camomile from an upstairs room in one of the houses that overlooked the meadow. A girl, maybe her own age or a little older, was standing by the window and watching intently as they trotted round the field. Because the houses were so close, Mandy could see her face quite clearly. Something about the girl's expression made her feel uneasy. She had been going to wave, because she was enjoying the ride so much and wanted to share her high spirits, but now she dropped her hand awkwardly.

Just then, Camomile stumbled over a tussock of grass and Mandy lost her stride. By the time she looked back up at the window again, the girl had vanished.

Four

'Well, thank you, Camomile,' Mandy said, patting the horse's warm, damp neck as she held her by the reins. 'That was great!'

Camomile gave a little shake of her mane and whinnied a couple of times, as if to say that it had been a pleasure.

'You could tell she was really pleased to get out and stretch her legs properly,' James said, swinging his leg over the saddle before slithering down to the ground and landing with a thump. 'Oof! That was further than I thought.'

The two of them had taken it in turns to ride

Camomile, with the one who wasn't riding jogging alongside, or waiting at the edge of the bridle-path while horse and rider took off for a circuit on their own. Camomile had seemed to love every minute of her time outside the paddock.

'There must be someone round here who'd love to exercise her,' Mandy said, holding the mare still while James took off her saddle. 'If only we could find out who!' She looked into Camomile's intelligent brown eyes and stroked her soft muzzle. The mare blew softly down her nose and nuzzled Mandy's fingers.

And then suddenly Mandy remembered the girl who'd been watching them out of the window earlier. Which house had it been? She stared across, trying to remember. A quick flicker of movement at one of the first-floor windows caught her eye, but when she looked more closely, nobody was there. Perhaps she'd imagined it.

'There was someone watching us earlier on,' she told James when he'd come back from the stable. 'A girl, in one of those houses in Green Lane that back on to the field.'

'Do you think she might be interested in riding?'

James asked, settling his glasses back on his nose. 'She's certainly in the right place to help with Camomile. It would be perfect!'

'I'm not sure,' Mandy replied doubtfully, remembering the sense of unease she'd felt before. 'She looked a bit – I don't know – disapproving, somehow. Not particularly friendly, anyway. Still, it might be worth seeing if Mrs Tandy knows who she is.'

She took off Camomile's bridle and slipped the headcollar over her nose. 'You need sponging off, I think,' she said, running her fingers lightly over the dark patches of sweat on the mare's flanks. 'I'll get a bucket and sponge from the stable and we can make you more comfortable.'

After giving Camomile a good rub down, they walked her quietly round the meadow until her coat had dried in the sun. When everything had been put away neatly and they were back at the house, having a snack of apple juice and biscuits, Mandy asked Mrs Tandy if she knew who the mysterious girl might be.

Mrs Tandy frowned. 'Let me see,' she said. 'I know most of the people in Green Lane who back on to the field. The Bradshaws have two girls, but they're much older – besides, they're away on holiday at the moment.' Then her face cleared. 'Got it!' she exclaimed. 'There's a new family who arrived a few months ago. From Wales, I think the mother said. Such a nice, friendly woman! She's on her own – divorced or separated, I believe. I took round a cake when they'd just moved in. Three children, two younger boys and a girl who's about your age. That must be who you saw.'

'We wondered if maybe she'd like to ride Camomile,' James explained, helping himself to another flapjack. 'She's close by, isn't she? And it looks as though she's interested in horses.'

'Oh no, I don't think so,' Mrs Tandy replied surprisingly firmly, topping up their glasses from a large jug of juice.

'She wouldn't be a stranger, though,' Mandy said, deciding the idea was worth a chance. 'After all, you've already met her mother.'

'No, it's not that,' Mrs Tandy said, dropping her voice a couple of notches as if she were afraid her neighbours might overhear. 'The poor girl has quite a bad limp. I didn't want to ask what the problem was, but I think riding would be out of the question.'

'Oh, what a shame.' Mandy said. She immediately began to feel quite differently about the girl. There was probably nothing better she'd have liked than to be riding Camomile in Mandy's place – perhaps that was why she had been staring at them so fiercely. It must be hard, watching other people having fun and knowing you couldn't join in. Mandy tried to imagine herself in the same situation, and felt a deep pang of sympathy.

The next afternoon, Mandy cycled home from school as fast as she could, all thoughts of Camomile and the girl at the window far from her mind. Sarah, the new practice nurse, would be coming to the end of her first day at Animal Ark and she couldn't wait to meet her. It would be fun to have a new face around at the surgery, and Mandy felt sure she and Sarah would have a lot to talk about. Mandy could always spend hours chatting about animals!

The waiting area at the surgery was crowded with pets and their owners. Jean Knox, the receptionist, was looking particularly harassed as she tried to deal with a queue of people at her desk.

'I only want to buy this cat collar,' called out a large, red-faced woman, waving her purse in the air. 'I can't see why on earth it should take so long.'

'Oh, Mandy, there you are!' Jean said in relief. 'Perhaps you could . . . ?'

'Sure,' Mandy said, slipping behind the counter and taking the lady's money for the collar. The next person in the queue was only asking which boarding kennels the surgery recommended, so she was able to help them too, and a couple more just wanted dried dog food. Before long, the queue had disappeared and order was restored.

'Thanks, dear,' Jean said gratefully, fanning her face with a leaflet advertising a new flea treatment.

'That's OK.' Mandy smiled. She took a quick look round at the animals that were waiting to be seen. There were quite a few cats, as usual, a couple of rabbits in a carrying cage and several dogs. She recognised one of them: Antonia was sitting there with her owner, Mrs Platt. The little poodle had had a terrible start in life – she'd been tied to a tree when she was only a puppy and left to starve. Luckily, she'd been rescued and had eventually recovered completely. Amazingly, she didn't seem to bear any ill will towards humans for the awful treatment she'd suffered, and had grown into a friendly, affectionate dog.

'Hello, Mrs Platt,' Mandy said, coming to sit beside her. 'How's Antonia? There's nothing wrong, is there?'

'Oh no, dear,' Mrs Platt said quickly. 'We've just come for her yearly booster. She's the picture of health, I'm delighted to say.' She stroked Antonia's curly white coat. The poodle looked up adoringly and licked her owner's fingers with a clean pink tongue. 'Mind you, we have been sitting here rather a long time,' Mrs Platt added, glancing at her watch. 'Things seem to be moving very slowly today.'

'We've got a new practice nurse to fill in while Simon's away,' Mandy explained. 'Perhaps that's why there's a hold-up.'

At that moment, they heard a loud crash from behind the closed door of one of the treatment rooms. Everyone looked up in alarm and, from behind the counter, Jean raised her eyebrows inquiringly at Mandy.

'Perhaps I'd better go and investigate,' Mandy said to Mrs Platt. She hurried over to the door and knocked a couple of times before opening it gently.

Her father was crouching down, picking up surgical instruments from a pile on the floor beside an overturned steel tray. A girl with brown curly hair in a dark green nurse's uniform kneeled beside him, apologising desperately as she tried to help.

'It's all right, Sarah,' Mr Hope was saying as Mandy came in. 'Really, I can manage. Look, why don't you take Tibbles and Mrs Hayward out to settle up with Jean?' A baleful-looking cat was being loaded into a wicker basket by his owner.

'Is there anything I can do?' Mandy offered, not wanting to get in the way.

'Oh, hello, love,' said her father, looking relieved and getting to his feet. 'Meet Sarah, our stand-in nurse! And Sarah, this is my daughter, Mandy. She probably knows as much about the place as we do.'

Sarah gave Mandy a quick smile. 'Hi there,' she

said, as she showed Mrs Hayward and Tibbles out. She looked hot and flustered and a bit dishevelled.

'How's it going?' she asked her father when Sarah had left the room and they were both crouched on the floor, clearing up the mess.

'Not bad, I suppose,' her father sighed. 'Sarah's a sweet girl and I'm sure she'll turn out to be a good nurse in the end. But she *is* rather slow, and she seems very accident-prone. That's the second time she's knocked over the tray of instruments!'

'Don't worry, Dad,' Mandy reassured him. 'I'm sure it's just because she's new and doesn't know her way round the surgery yet.'

'I hope you're right,' Mr Hope replied gloomily. 'Otherwise we'll be in for a rather trying three weeks!'

Over the next few days, the words, 'Never mind, Sarah!' were often to be heard around Animal Ark. She did seem to have a habit of dropping things, or knocking them over, or putting them in a safe place and then forgetting where it was.

Mandy found her parents in the kitchen one evening, having a quiet chat about the temporary nurse.

'I'm sure it's just a matter of confidence,' Mrs Hope said, leaning back in her chair. 'If she has one little accident, it seems to set off a whole chain of them. I think she gets nervous which makes her more clumsy. Still, she's ever so gentle with the animals.'

'And she's popular with their owners, too,' Mandy said, coming to sit down at the table and join in the conversation. She'd got to know Sarah a little and liked her, so she was keen to put in a good word. 'She always manages to cheer them up if they're worried, and she explains exactly what's going on with their pets. Gran and Grandad thought she was lovely when they brought Smoky in for his check-up.' Mandy smiled to herself. It had been great to see Smoky back to his normal lively self, and she felt sure he now had the cleanest teeth of any cat in Yorkshire.

'I know, you're right,' Mr Hope said, scratching his beard. 'It's just that everything seems to take twice as long as it used to, and people are getting fed up with waiting.'

'It makes you realise how much we've come to depend on Simon,' Emily Hope said thoughtfully.

'He does so many things without being asked. But then, Sarah's still learning, so she's bound to need a lot more supervision. Never mind – she'll get there eventually. We'll just have to be patient.'

'Come on, I *have* been trying,' Mr Hope said, jumping up from the table. 'Anyway, I'm off for a jog before it gets too dark.'

'Perhaps I could help you some more in the surgery,' Mandy said to her mother, picking up the threads of their conversation after her dad had left the room.

'Oh, you're busy enough as it is,' Mrs Hope replied. 'What with schoolwork and everything else you take on. Remind me, love, when are you exercising Camomile again? Do you need a lift?'

'On Saturday afternoon, after morning surgery,' Mandy said. 'And it's OK, thanks, Mum, James's dad's going to take us over there this time.'

She looked out of the window. The evenings were drawing in, and dusk was falling earlier and earlier. Shortly, there wouldn't be enough time to get to Mrs Tandy's in the afternoon and take Camomile out for a decent ride. They really ought to try and help find someone else to exercise her soon. She couldn't bear to think of the mare waiting all alone in the field for somebody to come and ride her.

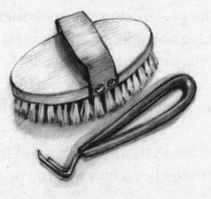

Five

Saturday morning surgery was nearly over when Mandy spotted John Hardy sitting in the waiting-room, a large cardboard box on his lap. She and James were friends with John, though they only really saw him in the holidays as he went to boarding school. Mandy went over to talk to him, hoping that there was nothing the matter with Button and Barney. She knew how fond he was of the two adorable brown rabbits.

'Hi, John! Don't tell me you're still on holiday,' she greeted him.

'Hello, Mandy,' he replied in his precise voice.

'Yes, I'm lucky – we don't go back till next week.'

Everything about John was neat and tidy – even his jeans looked as though they'd been ironed. Today, though, he was looking worried and Mandy noticed there were pieces of straw stuck to his T-shirt.

'Is everything OK with Button and Barney?' she asked, jamming her hands into the pockets of her white coat.

'Well, actually, it's Barney,' John said, opening the lid of the box more widely so Mandy could see in. The male rabbit was sitting hunched in the box, ears drooping. Mandy didn't need to look at Barney's runny nose and watery eyes to see that he was feeling miserable.

'Poor little thing,' she said sympathetically. 'How long has he been like this?'

'Well, he started sneezing yesterday,' John said, 'and then he suddenly got much worse this morning. I checked his symptoms in my book on rabbits and, from what I can make out, it looks like he might have snuffles. What do you think?'

'Hmm, possibly,' Mandy said cautiously. 'Let's see what Dad says.'

Privately, she agreed with John – it did look like Barney had snuffles, and she could see why he was worried. It was a disease that could be fatal if it wasn't caught in time. All the same, it would be best to leave the diagnosis up to her father. She'd heard both her parents grumble about owners who decided *they* knew what was wrong with their pets and wouldn't be told otherwise.

It turned out that John was quite right, though. 'Yes, he's got snuffles all right,' said her father, looking at the thermometer after he'd taken Barney's temperature. 'See that, Sarah? Nearly 42°C. Rabbits have higher temperatures than we do, but that's way too high. And look at the fur on his front legs – it's all matted from where he's been wiping his nose.'

'Poor old Barney,' Sarah said, looking down at the rabbit John was holding securely on the table. 'I'll get the antibiotic ready. Shall we give him lincomycin?'

'No, no, no!' Mr Hope exclaimed. 'That's OK for most other animals, but definitely not rabbits! It poisons them.'

'Oh, sorry,' Sarah said, flushing bright red. 'Of

course, I remember now. We covered that last term. Sorry!'

She dropped the bottle she'd just picked up, and when Mandy scrambled to help her retrieve it, they cracked heads together painfully.

'Oh, sorry!' Sarah said yet again, rubbing her forehead.

'That's OK,' Mandy replied, wincing with pain. She could tell the mistake had made Sarah feel flustered and upset.

'This antibiotic would be better,' Mr Hope said, picking another bottle off the shelf. 'Here, you hold Barney while I give him the dose.'

John stroked his rabbit reassuringly while Sarah held him still.

'How's Button?' Mandy asked, as her father injected the antibiotic carefully into Barney's side. 'Is she showing any of the same symptoms?'

'Not yet,' John replied. 'I separated them when Barney started sneezing, in case he had anything contagious.'

'That was a good idea,' Mr Hope said approvingly. 'All the same, I think we'd better keep him here at Animal Ark for a couple of days. Snuffles can spread like wildfire.'

'The only thing is, I have to go back to school on Tuesday,' John told them. 'Do you think he'll be better by then?'

'I should think so,' Mr Hope replied. 'We'll keep him in over the weekend and see how he responds to treatment. With a bit of luck, you'll be able to collect him on Monday afternoon.'

'Oh, good,' John said. 'I'd feel happier if he was safely home before I go off to school again. Not that he won't be safe here, of course,' he added hastily. 'You know what I mean.'

'Of course.' Mr Hope smiled. 'Don't worry, we'll

take good care of Barney for you.'

After John had said goodbye to Barney and left, Mandy helped Sarah take the rabbit down to the residential unit. Luckily, there weren't any other rabbits staying there – only a Yorkshire terrier, recovering from an operation to remove a fragment of bone that he'd swallowed.

Sarah put a heating pad in one of the cages to keep Barney warm and covered it with a blanket. Mandy noticed that the student nurse was still unsettled by what had happened in the treatment room.

'I can't believe I nearly gave this poor rabbit lincomycin,' she said gloomily. 'How could I have forgotten it would be toxic for him?'

'But Dad would never have let you use it without checking first,' Mandy reassured her. 'He and Mum are here to keep an eye on everything, so you don't need to worry. Don't be too hard on yourself – you didn't do it deliberately!'

'I know, but it feels like I'm making a mess of everything,' Sarah said. 'Dropping things, and getting in a muddle all the time. I think you and John knew more about treating Barney than I did!'

Mandy tried to think of something positive to say. 'Dad said to me once that if you don't make mistakes, you never learn,' she said, after a few seconds' thought.

Sarah gave a hollow laugh. 'Well, in that case I'm certainly bound to learn a lot!' she said. 'I just hope your mum and dad don't throw me out before I've picked up enough experience to help me pass my exams.'

'Of course they won't,' Mandy said, wishing she could find a way to cheer her up. 'Come on, I'm sure you'll sail through them. Who knows? If I can pass too, maybe one day we might end up working together!'

Mandy only had time to grab a quick lunch after surgery before James and his father arrived to pick her up on the way to Mrs Tandy's. When they arrived at the bungalow, they caught sight of the elderly lady sitting by the window, watching out for them. She waved and got to her feet immediately to open the door. After a quick chat with Mr Hunter, she ushered Mandy and James into the house.

'Oh, I'm so glad to see you both!' she said. 'And

Camomile will be, too. She's been standing there all morning with her head hanging over the gate, just as though she was waiting for you.'

'I'm sorry we can't come more often,' Mandy said, feeling guilty for a second. 'I know we don't visit regularly enough to be much use to you – or Camomile.'

'It's just too far for us to get here in the week,' James added. 'And I'm playing football most Sundays now, too.'

'I quite understand. It's very good of you to come at all,' Mrs Tandy said briskly, opening the French windows. 'I've decided to try and find someone local to exercise Camomile, even if I have to advertise. Laura's got a phone at last, and I had a long conversation with her last night. She agreed that Camomile needs to be ridden regularly.'

'She does seem to enjoy going out,' Mandy said. 'Besides, she's such a lovely horse to ride, it's a pity to let her go to waste.'

They walked down the garden to the field. There was Camomile with her head over the gate, just as Mrs Tandy had described. She neighed a couple of times when she saw them, then took off round the meadow in a canter.

'Look at her,' James said. 'You can tell she can't wait to get going.'

'Well, I'll leave you to it,' Mrs Tandy said. 'Have a wonderful time! And come up to the house for a drink and some cake when you're finished.'

'We will,' Mandy promised, following James through the gate.

It was much quicker to groom and tack Camomile up now they knew where everything was, and soon James was riding her round the field to work off some energy before taking her out on the road. Mandy sat on an upturned bucket by the stable and watched them, admiring the mare's graceful, easy action. Suddenly, she caught her breath. There was the girl at the window again! She was standing in the very same place, her gaze fixed on James and Camomile as they trotted past.

This time, Mandy felt as though she had to do something. Carefully, she counted along the number of back gardens in Green Lane to work out which house the girl lived in.

'I'll be back in a minute,' she called to James. 'Don't go off without me!'

Then she strode over to the gate that opened on to the road and let herself out of the field. It was unnerving, the way this girl was watching them, and she was determined to find out why she kept doing it.

Before she could give herself time to think better of it, Mandy marched up the front path of what she felt sure was the right house, and rang the doorbell. She could hear the sound of children playing somewhere inside, and then footsteps coming down the hall towards the door. For an instant, her confidence faltered and she felt like turning back – but it was too late now.

The door was flung open by a tall woman with short dark hair, wearing leggings and a baggy T-shirt. 'Hello!' she said, looking at Mandy inquiringly.

'Hello,' Mandy replied. She took a deep breath and then began. 'We've come to ride the horse in the field behind your house – me and my friend, that is –'

'Oh yes,' the woman said, her face lighting up in a smile. 'She's beautiful, isn't she? I keep telling

Rhian she should go down and give her an apple.'

Good! So it is the right house, Mandy thought to herself. *That's a relief.*

'It's Mrs Tandy's field, isn't it?' the woman went on. 'Does she own the horse too?'

'It's her daughter's,' Mandy explained, 'but she's gone away for a while and Mrs Tandy's looking after Camomile. She needs help exercising her, though, so James and I are helping out when we can. My name's Mandy Hope.'

'And I'm Claire Jones,' said the woman, sticking out her foot and neatly fielding a football which had come shooting down the hall. The ball was closely followed by a couple of small boys with the same dark hair as their mother. 'And these two horrors are Glyn and Huw.' She tossed them the ball back, saying sternly, 'Not in the house, boys! How many times do I have to tell you? Football in the garden, OK?'

'I was wondering whether your daughter would like to come and meet Camomile,' Mandy went on. 'The thing is, we've seen her watching us. Does she like horses?'

'Oh, yes – Rhian loves them,' Mrs Jones said enthusiastically. 'She's been telling me she's grown out of riding, but I don't know where that silly idea came from. She just needs a little encouragement to get to know Camomile – that's all! Let me call her down and we can put it to her.'

Mandy clenched her fingers rather nervously in her pockets. For a second, she wondered why she'd come to the house in the first place. Perhaps it would have been better to have left things well alone.

After Mrs Jones had shouted 'Rhian!' a couple of times, a girl with long dark hair came slowly down the stairs. She walked awkwardly, carefully holding on to the banister and putting most of her weight on her left side. When she reached the last step she stood there and looked down at them warily, as though she didn't want to come too close.

'Rhian, this is Mandy Hope,' her mother said encouragingly. 'She and her friend have been riding the horse in Mrs Tandy's field.'

'I thought maybe you'd like to come and say hello to her,' Mandy offered. 'And you could come with us when we take her out, if you want. You don't have to ride her or anything. We take turns on Camomile, so there's always someone walking.'

'What do you think, Rhian?' Mrs Jones said, smiling hopefully at her daughter. 'That sounds like fun, doesn't it? Wouldn't you like to go with them?'

Rhian shot Mandy a long, cool look. 'I can't come right now,' she said abruptly. 'I'm a bit busy at the moment. Sorry.'

'Oh, go on – why not, love?' said her mother, reaching up and giving Rhian's arm a little shake. 'You used to be so interested in horses!'

'Yes, I *used* to be,' Rhian said deliberately. 'But I'm not any more, OK? I wish you'd just accept the fact! Give it a rest, will you?' And with that, she turned and stomped back up the stairs.

Mrs Jones looked embarrassed. 'I'm so sorry,' she said to Mandy, shrugging her shoulders. 'But thanks for making the effort. It was really kind of you.'

'Oh, that's OK,' Mandy replied. 'I just thought I'd ask.'

There didn't seem any more to be said, so she wished Mrs Jones goodbye and walked back down the path, her cheeks burning. There was no need for Rhian to have been so rude: staring at her as though she was something unpleasant. She was only trying to be friendly, after all. Well, she certainly wouldn't try again!

Six

'A bit busy!' Mandy snorted as she marched along beside James and Camomile. 'If she's so busy, why does she spend all her time staring out of the window?' She was still smarting from the brush-off Rhian had given her.

'Calm down,' James said. 'It's probably just as well she's not coming if she's so touchy. It was nice of you to offer, though.' He gazed out over the fields on either side of the road. 'It's great on horseback, isn't it?' he went on. 'You get a much better view.'

Mandy looked round. Her eyes had been fixed

on the ground as she walked crossly down the lane towards the bridle-path, and only now did she notice that the misty morning had turned into a beautiful afternoon. The sun was warm on her back, but a crisp tang in the air warned that autumn was just round the corner. The bushes were crimson with hawthorn berries and birds were singing loudly in the trees, claiming their territories for winter.

'You're right,' she said, smiling up at James. 'It's lovely to be out here with Camomile, and I'm not going to spoil it! After all, if Mrs Tandy finds someone else to exercise her then we won't have many more rides like this.'

By the time she'd had a turn cantering along the bridle-path, Camomile's hooves thudding on the hard earth, Mandy had forgotten about Rhian Jones altogether. So it was quite a shock to see her, leaning against the gate, when she and James arrived back at the meadow after their ride.

'Hello,' Mandy said warily, looking down from her seat on Camomile's broad back.

'Shall I open the gate?' Rhian asked, despite the fact that James was right there and about to do it himself.

'OK. Thanks,' Mandy said, realising that Rhian was trying to make up for her rude behaviour earlier.

'Do you want a hand?' James asked, springing forward to help as Rhian struggled with the awkward wooden gate.

'No, it's all right. I can manage,' she replied sharply, flushing with exertion as she dragged it across the grass.

Mandy rode Camomile through the gap, then swung her leg over the saddle and dismounted. She and James looked at each other in silence, not sure what to expect, while Rhian pushed the gate shut before limping over towards them.

'Look, I wanted to say sorry,' she began, slightly out of breath. 'I didn't mean to be rude just now. It was nice of you to ask me to come along.'

Mandy was completely taken aback. Rhian seemed like a different girl. 'That's all right,' she replied after a moment. 'We weren't trying to force you or anything. We just thought you might like to get to know Camomile. This is my friend James, by the way.'

Rhian said hello to James and glanced quickly at the horse. She didn't seem to want to stroke or pat her. 'The thing is, I used to ride a lot,' she said, 'but I really don't want to any more. My mum just keeps going on and on about me taking it up again. I wish she'd leave it alone – she's driving me mad!'

'So the last thing you wanted was me turning up and inviting you over,' Mandy said, beginning to understand why their earlier conversation had been so tense.

'Yes, but you weren't to know that,' Rhian admitted. 'There was no need for me to bite your head off. Sorry!' And she smiled at them. A quick, very guarded smile, but still a smile.

'That's OK,' Mandy replied. She could see how proud Rhian was. It probably cost her a lot to apologise, and Mandy appreciated the effort she was making. Besides, she wasn't one to bear a grudge. 'Anyway, I think your mum got the worst of it!' she added.

'I know, but I've already sorted it out with her,' Rhian said ruefully. She shook her head and added fiercely, 'I can't stand being told to do things "for my own good", that's all. Why can't *I* be the one to decide what's good for me?'

'Mandy only came round because we thought you were interested and you lived so close by,' James put in. 'Mrs Tandy needs some help with Camomile and here you are, right on her doorstep.'

'Well, like I told you, I've given up riding for ever,' Rhian said, with that stubborn, closed look coming over her face again. 'And it's not just some "silly idea" I've come up with.' Then she flushed, realising she'd given away the fact that she'd been listening to Mandy and her mother talking together.

Camomile stamped at the ground and jerked her head against Mandy's grip. It was time to rub her down, but Mandy didn't want break up the conversation just yet. She had to find out exactly why Rhian was so determined not to ride any more.

'Did you have a bad fall?' she asked, wondering if Rhian had simply lost her confidence.

The older girl shook her head. 'No, I was born like this,' she said. 'It's a mild form of cerebral palsy. My right side doesn't work too well, though I can do most things with my left hand.'

Mandy was horrified at the misunderstanding. 'Oh no, I didn't mean that,' she said hastily, blushing bright red. 'I thought you might have stopped riding because you'd had a scare, that's all.'

'It's OK, don't worry,' Rhian said easily. 'I don't mind talking about what's wrong with me. Other people sometimes get embarrassed, but I'm used to it by now.'

Camomile began to toss her head again, grinding her teeth against the metal bit in her mouth. Rhian gave the mare another quick look. 'Listen, it's a long story,' she said quietly, 'and you'd better get Camomile untacked now. Maybe I'll see you another time.' With that, she turned to leave.

'Hang on,' Mandy said, calling her back. 'We're going to Mrs Tandy's house for a bit when we've finished here. Why don't you come round in half an hour or so? I'm sure she wouldn't mind.'

James looked at Mandy in surprise, and there was a slightly awkward pause. Then he quickly added, 'Yes, why don't you? We're going to have something to drink and there's a cake, too – home-made!'

Rhian looked at them, considering the idea. She obviously didn't do anything without thinking about it carefully first. Eventually she said, 'OK, if you really think she won't mind. My brothers have got some friends round and the house is full of screaming kids. It would be good to get out for a while.'

'Well, she wasn't so bad!' James said, after Rhian had gone and they were leading Camomile back to her stable. 'And you've changed your mind about her, haven't you? I couldn't believe it when you invited her over to Mrs Tandy's later on!'

'Yes, you made that clear enough,' Mandy said, making a face at him over the saddle as she ran up the stirrup iron on her side. 'Well, why shouldn't we be friendly? Besides, aren't you curious? There must be more to this than Rhian's admitting. If she's so sure she doesn't want to ride any more, then why was she watching us all the time? And she was so strange with Camomile! She hardly looked at her.'

'Come on, don't make a mystery out of everything,' James said good-naturedly, unbuckling the girth and letting it swing down for Mandy to catch. 'Rhian knew we'd seen her staring at us, didn't she? Maybe she's trying to prove that she's not really interested, after all.'

'I'm sure she *is*, though,' Mandy pondered. She flipped the loose end of the girth over the saddle, but paused before she heaved it off to add, 'It was just as if she couldn't bear to *let* herself look at Camomile or touch her, though she really wanted to. No, there's something strange about all this, James – and I'm going to find out what it is!'

'So, did you have a horse of your own?' Mandy asked Rhian carefully, as they sat eating chocolate cake on a bench in Mrs Tandy's garden. Mrs Tandy had been more than happy to let them all go outside, so they wouldn't drop crumbs on her cream living-room carpet.

Rhian shook her head, her mouth full. 'No, I went to a riding-school every week,' she said after she'd swallowed a mouthful of cake. 'I began to get interested in horses when I was about eight, but the doctors told me I wouldn't ever be able to ride. Shows you how much they know! After

I'd had operation to loosen up the tendons in my right leg and arm, I started going to a Riding for the Disabled centre near where we lived in Wales.'

'I bet they have a centre round here too,' James said. 'If you contacted the main Riding for the Disabled offices, they could give you a list of addresses.'

'Oh, for goodness' sake!' Rhian exclaimed. 'How many times do I have to tell everyone? I don't *want* to start riding again, OK?' She stood up and brushed some crumbs off her jeans, and Mandy shot James a warning frown behind her back.

'Sorry,' James mumbled, blushing as he drank some apple juice.

Rhian looked at him, and then abruptly sat down again. 'It's all right,' she said. 'I suppose I am a bit touchy. When you have a disability, you get so sick of people trying to tell you what to do all the time. My mind works perfectly well, thank you very much. I can make my own decisions.'

They were all quiet for a moment, and then Mandy noticed Camomile amble up to the fence at the bottom of the garden and put her head over the gate. She neighed a couple of times before wandering off again to graze.

'Isn't she lovely?' Mandy smiled, forgetting for an instant that Camomile was part of the subject Rhian probably wanted to avoid.

'Yes, she is,' Rhian agreed, gazing at the mare as the sunshine gleamed on her smooth golden coat. Then she added, almost absent-mindedly, 'She has such a look of Polo about her.'

Mandy looked at her, not sure whether she dared to ask who Polo was in case Rhian thought she was prying. James obviously felt the same, but neither of them could think of anything else to say.

'Polo was the pony I used to ride at the centre,' Rhian explained, breaking the silence. 'We got to know each other so well that they let me ride him all the time, and I looked after him, too. He was great! The kind of horse who knows what you want him to do before you've even given the command.'

'You must have been sad to leave him behind,' Mandy said.

Rhian sighed. 'No, he wasn't there any more by the time we moved,' she said, and something about the tone of her voice made Mandy hold her breath. She felt as though they were coming to the heart of the mystery.

'What happened?' she asked, trying to prompt Rhian as gently as she could.

'He had colic,' Rhian said slowly. She took a deep breath. 'I spent a lot of time looking after him when he was in pain, but the attacks just got worse and worse. In the end, he had to be put down.'

'That's terrible!' James exclaimed.

Mandy was so shocked, she couldn't think what to say for a moment. 'How sad,' she said eventually, struggling to find the right words. 'You must miss him so much.'

Rhian nodded. 'Yes, I do,' she said quietly, biting her lip. 'He was my best friend. That's one of the best things about animals, isn't it? You can tell them what you like and they never try to give you advice, or criticise you, or tell you to do things for your own good. They just listen. Whenever things got me down, I'd go and talk to Polo, and I always felt better afterwards. It didn't really matter that he couldn't understand what I was saying.'

She smiled sadly and added, 'I used to think he did understand me, though. He'd look at me with those big brown eyes and nuzzle my shoulder as if he was telling me everything would turn out all right. But it didn't – not for him, anyway.'

Mandy felt a lump come in her throat. There were tears in Rhian's eyes and she felt desperately sorry for her, though she knew better than to say so.

'Couldn't you talk to Camomile instead?' James suggested timidly. 'She's such a beautiful horse – you're bound to fall in love with her once you get to know her.'

'I know. That's just the problem!' Rhian said fiercely, getting awkwardly to her feet again and turning her back on the field as she looked down at Mandy and James. 'I'd fall in love with her and then something would happen! Mrs Tandy would sell her, or her daughter would decide to take her away, or maybe she'd get sick like Polo did.' She folded her arms and glared at them. 'I'm not going anywhere near her – it's just not worth the risk! If you don't get involved in the first place, you can't be hurt if things go wrong.'

Mandy stared back at Rhian in dismay. That had

to be one of the saddest things she'd ever heard anyone say.

Seven

Mandy and James were both quiet in the car on the way home. Mrs Tandy chattered on while she drove, but Mandy found it hard to concentrate on the conversation. She kept thinking about Rhian, and how determined she was not to have anything to do with Camomile. It was so frustrating. Mandy felt certain Rhian would be ten times happier if she was riding again, rather than being cooped up in her bedroom all day. And there was Camomile, practically living in her back garden and needing the exercise! The mare was so sweet and gentle that Rhian would surely be able to manage her easily. Mandy sighed. There had to be a way to bring them together, if only she could think of it . . .

She told her parents all about her dilemma while they were eating that evening.

'Well, one thing's clear,' her father said, when she'd finished talking. 'You're going to have to let Rhian make up her own mind. The answer might seem obvious to you, but she's come to a different decision and you'll have to respect that.'

'So what do you think I should do?' Mandy asked, munching on a slice of pizza. Saturday-night suppers were always more relaxed than weekday meals – everyone seemed to have more time and there weren't so many chores to be done.

'Why don't you try and get to know Rhian a little better?' her mother advised, helping herself to garlic bread. 'You've only met her once, after all. She's just moved into the area and she's probably quite lonely. If you carry on calling round after you've taken Camomile out, you might find she becomes interested in spite of herself. But I wouldn't try to force anything, like Dad says.'

'I suppose not,' Mandy said, pushing aside her

plate and wiping her fingers with a piece of paper towel. 'Anyway, Mrs Tandy's going to try and find someone to exercise Camomile in the week. She's going to contact a couple of riding-schools and see whether they can suggest anybody who'd be interested. We might not be going round there for much longer.'

She took her plate over to the sink and glanced up at the kitchen clock. There was a television programme she really wanted to watch that started in a few minutes, but she still had time to look in on the residential unit first.

'How's Barney doing?' she asked, leaning on the back of her father's chair. 'I haven't had a chance to see him yet.'

'Oh, he's much better already,' Mr Hope said, turning round with a smile. 'It's amazing how quickly antibiotics work.'

'Great!' Mandy said. 'John'll be pleased.'

Barney certainly looked much happier. His eyes were brighter and his nose wasn't streaming quite so much.

When John came round to visit on Sunday afternoon, Barney was looking better still. Mandy fixed up a run in the back garden and they let Barney spend some time outside in the sunshine. He sat there, nibbling the grass contentedly and looking like he was really enjoying the open air.

'He'll need to be on antibiotics for a few more days, but he can certainly go home tomorrow afternoon,' Mr Hope said, as John was about to leave.

'That's wonderful!' he replied, looking relieved. 'Is it OK if I come and pick him up about five? Dad's taking me into Walton to do some last-minute shopping, and I don't think we'll be back before then.'

'That's fine,' Mandy said. 'Isn't it, Dad? We'll have him ready for you.'

'Sarah and I will,' her mother corrected. 'Dad's vaccinating the dairy cows up at Sam Western's farm tomorrow afternoon, so we're taking surgery on our own. And *you'll* be doing your homework, Mandy Hope. You leave it far too late and then you're too tired to work properly.'

'OK, OK,' Mandy said, shrugging her shoulders guiltily as she remembered the schoolbag waiting upstairs in her bedroom.

* * *

The next day, James and Mandy cycled home from school together. James was a year younger than Mandy, so his class was working on topics she'd already covered. They were about to start a project on the Romans, and Mandy had a useful book at home she'd promised to lend him.

'Hang on a minute!' Mandy said as they came within sight of Animal Ark. 'What's Sarah doing out here?'

'She seems to be looking for something,' James said, squinting through his glasses. 'I wonder what it is?'

Sarah was crouching down by the side of the road, peering intently into the verge.

'What's up?' Mandy asked, skidding to a halt on some loose stones with James close behind her.

Sarah turned round, and Mandy could see at once that she'd been crying. 'It's Barney,' she said miserably. 'He's escaped!'

'Oh no!' Mandy gasped. 'When? How?'

'About an hour ago,' Sarah replied, staring back at the undergrowth. 'I took him out of the cage to give him some nose drops and he wriggled out of my grasp.'

'But how did he get outside?' James asked. 'Out of the unit, I mean.'

Sarah winced. 'I'd left the door open behind me,' she said, as though she could hardly bear to admit it even to herself. 'He ran off somewhere and vanished into thin air! Your mum's searching the garden now.'

'We'll help you look,' Mandy said immediately, and James nodded in agreement. 'Don't worry, Sarah – he probably hasn't gone far.'

'But afternoon surgery's starting in fifteen minutes,' Sarah said desperately. 'And John's meant to be picking Barney up at five! What if we haven't found him by then?'

'We can carry on hunting for him while you're working,' James reassured her. 'Between us, I'm sure we'll soon find him!'

Ten minutes later, though, there was still no sign of Barney. The three of them had walked up and down the lane, scanning the front gardens on either side. After that, they went through to the back garden to find out if Mrs Hope had seen any sign of the runaway. She was on her knees by the apple tree, holding back her red hair with one hand as she looked in the long grass, but she simply shook her head as they approached.

Mandy was getting very worried by now, though she did her best to hide it from Sarah. John had left Barney at Animal Ark, trusting that he would be looked after properly. It would be a terrible blow for everyone if anything happened to him while he was in the Hopes' care. What if a fox found him before they did? James began calling Barney's name, but a rabbit wasn't like a dog that would come running back to its owner. And the garden at Animal Ark certainly wasn't escape-proof. Barney could have wriggled through a gap in the hedge and gone anywhere by now!

'We'll have to start surgery, now, Sarah,' Mrs Hope said, looking at her watch as cars arriving with the first few appointments began pulling into the carpark. 'Mandy, can you and James carry on looking?'

'Of course we will,' Mandy promised. 'I bet we'll be back with Barney in our arms before you know it.'

Together, she and James began to go over every inch of the garden again. 'I'm sure he's not here any more,' James said eventually. 'Let's go back out to the lane and have another look there.'

'Oh, this is hopeless, James!' Mandy said, after they'd walked up and down the lane a couple more times. She stared at the seemingly endless row of front gardens, stretching away towards the main street in Welford. There were so many places for a rabbit to hide! Under bushes, behind cars, in porches, down side passages – not to mention inside the sheds and greenhouses in everyone's back garden. Barney could be anywhere, and John was meant to be picking him up in twenty minutes! They would never find him in time.

'Come on. Let's try and look at this logically,' James said, sitting down on the verge and settling his glasses firmly on his nose. 'We've got to think like Barney. Where would *we* go, if we were rabbits?'

Mandy couldn't help giggling at the thought of James and herself, hopping down the road with their noses twitching like Button and Barney. He was right, though. They needed a plan – searching aimlessly wasn't getting them anywhere.

'Well, Barney's been taken to a strange place, away from home,' she began, thinking out loud.

'But he's been cared for, so he won't be looking for food.'

'He needs to find somewhere safe,' James went on. 'Perhaps a burrow or a place he can hide. Do you think he might have come across a wild rabbit's hole and gone in there?'

Mandy looked doubtful. 'I don't think so,' she said. 'Rabbits are quite territorial – they know the smell of their own home. I remember John telling me that a rabbit won't shelter in a strange burrow, even if it's being chased by a fox.'

'Well, that's it, then!' James cried, jumping up. 'Of course!'

'What do you mean, "of course"?' Mandy asked, looking at him curiously.

'Don't you think Barney will have tried to go home? Back to the Fox and Goose?' James said excitedly, starting off down the road.

Mandy turned the idea over in her mind. She suddenly remembered what her grandfather had said about Smoky: 'Cats are more attached to places than to people.' Perhaps that applied to rabbits, too. And the more she thought about it, the more obvious it seemed that Barney would head for the safety of home.

'James, you're brilliant!' she said, hurrying after him. 'I don't know why we didn't think of that before!'

'Well, at least it's worth a try,' James said when Mandy had caught up. 'The only trouble is, what if John's come back from Walton and he's at the pub already? We can't exactly tell him what we're doing, can we?'

'Then we'll just have to make something up,' Mandy said firmly. 'Let's tackle one problem at a time!'

To their relief, the carpark at the Fox and Goose was completely empty. The pub wasn't due to open for another hour or so, and it looked like John and his father and stepmother were still out shopping.

'How are we going to get round the back into the beer garden, though?' Mandy asked James. 'That's where Barney will have gone if he's trying to get back to his hutch, isn't it? But, look – the door's locked!'

'Think about it, you dummy!' James told her. 'If *we* can't get in, Barney can't either. What's he going to do, fly over the wall?'

'Oh yes, of course,' Mandy replied, feeling

rather stupid. 'So, if he *has* gone back to the pub, he'll be here at the front.'

Her spirits sank as she looked round the deserted carpark. At first glance, there was no sign of Barney anywhere.

'Doesn't look hopeful, does it?' James said, echoing her thoughts. He wandered towards a narrow flowerbed, planted with low shrubs, that ran along one side of the carpark. It only took a couple of minutes to make sure that Barney wasn't hiding there, though.

'Just a minute!' Mandy said suddenly. She hurried off towards the porch by the front door, where Walter and his friend Ernie Bell enjoyed sitting when the pub was open.

'Where are you going?' James called. 'It's closed! You can't get inside.'

'I know,' Mandy called back over her shoulder. She was heading for a little wooden wheelbarrow next to the porch, which John's father had planted with bright petunias and busy Lizzies, matching the colourful hanging baskets on the wall. There was something in the wheelbarrow that shouldn't have been there! Mandy had spotted the tip of one velvety brown ear, sticking up in the middle of a clump of flowers. And as she came closer, she could make out a twitching black nose and one dark beady eye.

'Got you!' she exclaimed joyfully, grasping Barney tightly and hauling him out of the wheelbarrow. The rabbit did his best to look innocent, but half a pink petunia dangling out of his mouth gave the game away.

'You naughty bunny!' Mandy laughed, burying her face in Barney's soft fur. 'We've all been so worried about you!'

'That was in the nick of time,' James said, hurrying up to join her. 'Look who's just arrived!'

Mr Hardy's low green car had pulled into the carpark. John was sitting on the back seat, watching them.

'Explanation time,' James murmured, as John climbed out of the car and walked over towards them.

Mandy hastily pulled the petunia out of Barney's mouth and smiled innocently at John as he approached. 'We thought you'd probably be busy,' she said, holding the rabbit out to him. 'So we brought Barney back, to save you the trouble of coming over!'

'Thanks,' John smiled, taking the rabbit out of Mandy's arms. 'But wouldn't it have been easier to bring him in the box?' he went on, after he'd given Barney a cuddle. He looked at Mandy as though he was beginning to find the whole idea rather surprising.

'Yes, probably,' she replied, starting to hurry away before he could ask any more awkward questions. 'Never mind, we'll know next time! Oh, and we'll bring round the rest of his medicine later on this evening.'

'Fine!' John called back with a wave.

'Phew! That was a close one,' James said with a grin, as they hurried back to Animal Ark.

'You're telling me!' Mandy agreed. 'Still, I can't wait to see Sarah's face when she hears that Barney's safely home!'

Eight

When Mandy and James dashed into the reception area at Animal Ark, they saw Sarah talking to Jean behind the counter. She looked across at them hopefully, but her face fell when she saw they were empty-handed.

'It's all right!' Mandy said, hurrying over to share the good news. 'We found Barney outside the pub and gave him straight back to John! He doesn't know Barney ever went missing in the first place.'

Sarah stared at her for a few seconds, hardly able to believe what she was hearing. Then she gave a gasp of relief and hugged Mandy so tightly she could hardly breathe. 'Thank you, thank you!' she said over and over again, while Jean beamed delightedly in the background. Mrs Hope appeared at that moment to collect the next patient's notes, so James quickly filled her in on what had happened.

'Oh, thank goodness Barney's safe!' Emily Hope said, the strained look immediately disappearing from her face. 'I wouldn't have enjoyed telling John he'd gone missing. Now, Sarah – time to get back to work!'

'Yes, ma'am!' Sarah said, finally letting Mandy go. 'And I'll never lose another patient again – I promise.'

'You'd better not,' Mrs Hope replied severely, though a smile was hovering round the corners of her mouth. 'I don't think our reputation would ever recover!'

'Come on, let's go through to the house,' Mandy said to James, as the others went about their business. 'The Romans will feel like a doddle after all this excitement.' Now the search was over, she wanted to slump into a chair and not have to worry about anything else for the rest of the evening.

They stopped off in the kitchen for something to drink and a packet of crisps each, then went across the hall to the study. Mandy was running out of space on the shelves in her bedroom, so she'd started keeping her reference books in there.

'I'm sure it's somewhere on this shelf,' she muttered, running her finger along a line of books on one of the shelves that ran across three walls in the study. As well as her parents' veterinary textbooks, leather-bound volumes on local history and the countryside jostled for space with the latest scientific journals.

'It's like looking for a needle in a haystack,' James said, gazing at row upon row of titles.

'Or a rabbit in a wheelbarrow,' Mandy joked. 'Aha! Here we are!' She drew a thin paperback from the shelf and started rifling through the pages. 'See?' she said, showing it to James. 'There's a brilliant picture of a Roman soldier here, and they've got a section on the Coliseum a bit further on.'

'That's great,' James said, taking the book from her. 'It's exactly what I need! I've looked up Roman history on the Internet, but there's so much information it'll take me for ever to work through it.'

They were suddenly disturbed by the shrill ringing of the telephone, sounding very loud in the quiet room. When Mandy answered, she heard Mrs Tandy's voice on the other end of the line. It was obvious straight away that something was wrong.

'Oh, Mandy! Thank goodness you're in,' Mrs Tandy said hurriedly. 'I need to talk to you, if you've got a minute to spare. It's Camomile!'

'What's the matter?' Mandy asked urgently, her heart beginning to race. 'Has something happened?'

'She's got colic,' Mrs Tandy said, the words beginning to spill out so fast she stumbled over them. 'At least, I'm pretty sure that's what it is. First of all I noticed she hadn't finished her morning feed, and then this afternoon she started pawing at the ground. She seems very uneasy too – looking round at her stomach as though she knows something's wrong. I'm sure she's in pain.'

Mandy tried to keep calm. Colic could be a symptom of something serious, and she could tell that Mrs Tandy was extremely worried. It was

important that she didn't panic, though. 'Have you called the vet?' she asked next, looking into James's concerned face as she spoke. Quickly, she mouthed, 'Camomile – colic!' so he would have some idea what was going on.

'Yes, I have – just now,' came the answer. 'He's treating a cat that's been hit by a car, but he's coming to see Camomile as soon as he's finished. I just wish there was somebody to help me with her until he arrives. What if she gets worse? I don't suppose you'd be able to come, could you, dear?'

Mandy bit her lip, desperately trying to think of a way round the situation. There didn't seem any way they could possibly get to Mrs Tandy's house. Her father was out with the Animal Ark Land-rover, and her mother would be busy in surgery for another couple of hours at least.

'Hang on a second,' she said to Mrs Tandy, and put her hand over the telephone mouthpiece while she spoke to James. 'Camomile's got colic and the vet can't get there for a while. Is your dad home? Could he take us over?'

James shook his head. 'He won't be back with the car for ages,' he said. 'Sorry.'

'Look, I'm afraid we can't come over straight away,' Mandy told Mrs Tandy. 'But my dad will probably be back in an hour or so, and I'm sure he'd be happy to give us a lift then.'

'That's very kind,' Mrs Tandy said, though Mandy could hear the disappointment in her voice. 'I'm sorry to be such a nuisance! It's just that I feel so cut off, and I'm not quite sure what to do for the best.'

Mandy tried to remember what she knew about colic. 'I suppose you should keep Camomile company and try to reassure her till the vet arrives,' she said. 'Oh, and don't let her roll or thrash about. Walk her round if she looks like she might do herself any harm.'

'I'll do my best,' Mrs Tandy said bravely. 'If only she wasn't so big! Anyway, I'd better get back to her. Thanks for your help, dear.'

Mandy put the phone down, thinking she hadn't been much help at all. Mrs Tandy needed somebody beside her in the stable, not a faraway voice on the end of a telephone line. 'Poor Camomile!' she said to James. 'It's awful to think of her suffering – and Mrs Tandy sounded so upset. She needs someone to calm *her* down, too. Someone who knows a bit about horses and can give her some sensible advice.'

Then, as they looked at each other, the same idea struck both of them at exactly the same time.

'Rhian!' James exclaimed.

Mandy nodded. 'She looked after Polo when he had colic, so she must have some idea what to do,' she said. 'And she could be with Mrs Tandy in a matter of minutes.'

'Do you think she'd be willing to help, though?' James said doubtfully. 'She's made it very clear that she doesn't want to get involved. Besides, seeing a horse with colic is bound to bring back all sorts of painful memories.'

'But surely that's the one reason why she just *has* to help,' Mandy said, reaching for the phone directory. 'She couldn't possibly stand by if there was a risk of Camomile suffering like Polo did, could she?'

'I suppose it's worth a try,' James said. 'She can always say no.'

'She'd better not!' Mandy replied, turning to the right place in the phone book. There were hundreds of Joneses, and it took her a while to check all the addresses. 'Come on, come on!' she muttered, running her finger down the page. 'Where are the Joneses in Green Lane?' She felt as though Camomile was relying on them, and every second counted.

'No, no, no,' James said suddenly, taking the book out of her hands. 'They won't be in there, will they, if they only moved here a few months ago.'

'You're right!' Mandy said, picking up the phone. 'I'll ring Directory Enquiries instead. Oh, I hope they're listed!'

The operator answered immediately. He didn't

seem very impressed when Mandy gave him the name and then told him she didn't know which initial to look under.

'There are quite a few Joneses here,' he sighed. 'Don't you have any idea of the first name?'

Mandy's head whirled as she tried to remember. What had Mrs Jones said when she'd introduced herself on the doorstep? Something beginning with C, she thought it was, but she couldn't be sure. Christine? Kathleen? Kate? Would it be C or K?

Suddenly, she had it. 'C, for Claire!' she almost shouted into the phone. 'That's it! Mrs C. Jones, Green Lane. Oh, please – it's very important that we speak to her. But they only moved in a few months ago, so you might not have the number yet.'

'Our phone numbers are updated each evening,' the operator told her snootily. 'If Mrs C. Jones wants to be listed, she will be. Oh yes, here we are.'

Thank you, thank you, Mandy said to herself, as she wedged the telephone receiver under her chin and wrote down the Jones's number on the back of her hand.

Once she had dialled, the phone seemed to ring

on and on, while Mandy drummed her heels on the rug and thought she would explode with impatience. James leaned against the big wooden desk by the window, waiting to see what would happen.

Eventually, after what seemed like an eternity, Mrs Jones answered the phone.

'Oh, hello, Mandy,' she said cheerfully. 'Yes, Rhian's in. I'll just get her for you.' She put down the phone and called her daughter's name a couple of times. After another eternity, Rhian herself finally came on the line.

Mandy felt her mouth go dry. She'd spent so much effort trying to get hold of Rhian, she hadn't actually thought what she'd day to her when the time came. 'Rhian, there's a problem with Camomile,' she blurted in a rush. 'Mrs Tandy rang me just now. She's really worried about her!'

'What's that got to do with me?' Rhian replied coolly, after a few seconds' pause.

'We wondered if you could go round and help,' Mandy said. 'James and I would do it, but there's no way we can get over in time.' She took a breath, aware that everything was coming out wrong, and so started again more calmly. 'Rhian, Camomile has colic. Mrs Tandy's called the vet but he can't come straight away. She's all on her own with Camomile and she's not quite sure what to do. I know how you feel, but—'

'Look, I explained my reasons,' Rhian said icily, cutting her off. 'Can't you accept it and leave me alone? After everything I told you about Polo, I can't believe you're expecting me to get involved!'

'But that's why we thought of you,' Mandy said urgently, gripping the phone so tightly her fingers turned white. 'You looked after Polo when he had colic, didn't you? You must know all about it! Mrs Tandy's on her own and she really needs someone to give her some advice. Please, Rhian! Couldn't you help them, for Polo's sake? Camomile doesn't deserve to suffer any more than he did.'

There was another silence on the other end of the phone. Mandy held her breath; she didn't dare say anything else. It was up to Rhian now.

'You know how much you're asking, don't you?' she replied eventually. 'What if Camomile ends up in the same state as Polo? I've put all that behind me, Mandy. I can't face going through it again.'

'But the same thing won't happen to Camomile, I'm sure,' Mandy pleaded. 'Particularly not if you're there! She's never had colic before, and you can stop it turning into a serious attack. Please, Rhian!'

'I'm not sure,' Rhian said slowly. 'You'll have to give me some time to decide. Look, I'm not saying I *will* go round, but I'll think about it.'

'Thanks,' Mandy said. 'I know how hard this must be for you.'

The line went dead, and she carefully replaced the receiver. 'We'll have to wait for Rhian to make her mind up,' she told James, feeling completely drained. 'There's nothing else we can do. I just hope she doesn't take too long to decide!'

Nine

Mandy paced up and down the kitchen, listening out with half an ear in case the phone rang. She didn't want to call Mrs Tandy herself, in case she took her away from Camomile at just the wrong moment, but she was desperate to find out what was happening. Had Rhian gone over to help? Was Camomile getting better or worse? James had had to go home for his tea and she'd been left to worry on her own, so it was quite a relief when her father arrived back from Mr Western's farm.

'Dad, there you are!' she said, as his tired face

appeared at the door. 'I'm so glad to see you.'

'That's a nice welcome,' Mr Hope said, pulling out a chair and collapsing into it. 'Well, I reckon I've earned my supper today. Seventy-five cows vaccinated! Not bad for an afternoon's work.'

'Great,' Mandy agreed, filling up the kettle and switching it on. She knew better than to ask her father to drive her over to Mrs Tandy's house immediately. There was more chance he'd feel like it after a mug of tea.

The phone rang, and her father groaned. 'Don't worry, Dad. I'll get that,' Mandy told him, already on her way to answer the call. As she picked up the receiver, she felt her heart turn over at the sound of Mrs Tandy's voice.

'Mandy? Is that you, dear?'

'Yes, it's me!' Mandy said eagerly. 'How's everything going? How's Camomile?'

'Well, I think we've got things under control,' Mrs Tandy replied, sounding much less panicky than she had before.

Mandy felt relief flooding through every part of her body. 'Oh, that's good news!' she said, sinking into the chair. Then she sat bolt upright. 'Who's "we"?' she asked, fully taking in what Mrs

Tandy had said. 'Has the vet arrived?'

'No, dear, not yet. Rhian's here,' Mrs Tandy explained, and Mandy punched the air in a silent victory salute. 'She climbed over the fence at the bottom of their garden and came to help me. What an angel! She knows just what to do. Camomile was quite bad when she got here, but she calmed her right down. She's even managed to get her to take some bran mash!'

'Thank goodness for that,' Mandy said. 'Is she with Camomile now?'

'Oh, yes. She's going to look after her till the vet arrives,' Mrs Tandy replied. 'I'm at the window looking out for him now, so I thought I'd call to thank you while I had the chance. Rhian told me you'd rung and asked her to help.'

'Did you mind me telling her about Camomile?' Mandy asked. 'We couldn't think what else to do.'

'Of course not!' Mrs Tandy exclaimed. 'I don't know what I'd have done without her. Oh, just a minute, dear – I think the vet's arriving. I'd better go.'

'OK. Bye,' Mandy said, adding hurriedly, 'oh – would you mind if I came over to see Camomile –

if I can persuade Dad to give me a lift? He's just got home.'

'Of course – any time,' Mrs Tandy said. 'Goodbye, Mandy. And thanks again! You did exactly the right thing.'

'Great!' Mandy said quietly to herself as she hung up the phone. She was delighted that Rhian had finally decided to get involved, and not only for Camomile's sake. Perhaps looking after the mare and getting to know her would help Rhian accept Polo's death. She might say that she'd put it behind her, but Mandy didn't get the sense she'd really come to terms with losing him.

Back in the kitchen, her father was making himself a mug of tea. 'Dad . . .,' Mandy began. 'I was wondering . . .'

'I know that expression,' Mr Hope said with a grin, fishing the tea bag out of his mug and tossing it in the compost bucket. 'Come on, love – out with it! What are you after?'

Mandy couldn't help smiling back. She should have known better than to try and fool her dad. 'I was wondering if you could take me over to Mrs Tandy's,' she said, deciding to come clean. 'Camomile's got colic, but the vet's with her. And so is Rhian! We managed to persuade her to go round and help.'

'I'm not sure, Mandy. I've only just got in and it's quite late already,' her father said, taking a mouthful of tea. 'Even if we go straight away, we'll probably be late for supper.'

'Oh, please, Dad!' Mandy begged, putting her hand on his arm. 'We can leave Mum a note telling her where we've gone. I just *have* to find out how Camomile is, and I can't wait to see her and Rhian together!'

'All right,' Mr Hope sighed eventually. 'Camomile does mean a lot to you, doesn't she? Just let me finish my tea and then I'll take you. But we're only staying for half an hour at the most, OK?'

'Oh, thank you!' Mandy cried, flinging her arms round him. 'It'll be worth it, Dad – I promise!'

'Do you think there's a chance that Camomile could end up like Polo, the horse Rhian told us about?' Mandy asked her father on the way over to Mrs Tandy's. 'His colic got so bad he had to be put down in the end.'

'Well, it's not quite like that,' Mr Hope replied.

'Colic isn't a disease in itself – it's basically just a pain in the horse's stomach. That pain could be caused by anything from a tumour or a twisted gut, to a change in diet or some other kind of stress.'

'And is it easy to tell what *is* causing it?' Mandy asked.

'Sometimes,' her father said. 'I'm sure Mrs Tandy's vet will want to ask her about Camomile's feed, when she was last wormed, her exercise routine – that kind of thing. If it's a mild attack of colic, there probably isn't anything too serious behind it.'

'The trouble is, Camomile doesn't really have an exercise routine,' Mandy worried. 'I know Laura used to ride her regularly, but now she's having to make do with the odd ride from James and me at weekends.'

'That's not ideal,' her father said. 'If Camomile's feeling cooped up and frustrated, that could be why she's becoming colicky.'

His words confirmed what Mandy already knew. Mrs Tandy was going to have to find someone to exercise Camomile properly. Colic or no colic, it wasn't fair to keep her like this.

'Now you know I can't treat Camomile, don't you, love?' her father went on. 'If she's being seen by another vet, it wouldn't be right for me to interfere. I'm just your chauffeur for the evening.'

'Yes, I know.' Mandy smiled. 'And thanks, Dad. I really appreciate it.'

Soon they were pulling up outside Mrs Tandy's house. As they waited on the doorstep, Mandy felt her heart pounding. She was worried about Camomile and frightened that something might be seriously wrong, but at the same time she couldn't help feeling excited that Rhian was with her at last. She'd taken the first step; surely now she'd met Camomile properly, she wouldn't be able to help wanting to get to know her better?

Mrs Tandy came to the door with a middle-aged man whom Mandy assumed must be her vet. It turned out he and her dad knew each other, so they started chatting in the hall. Mandy drew Mrs Tandy aside and asked if she could go straight down to the field. As they didn't have much time, she couldn't bear to waste a second of it.

Camomile was lying on her side in the stable, on a thick bed of straw. Rhian sat cross-legged by her head, stroking the mare's fair mane

comfortingly. When she saw Mandy, she began scrambling to her feet.

'Don't get up,' Mandy said, coming to kneel beside her. 'How is she?'

'Better,' Rhian said briefly. 'The vet's given her some mineral oil and something for the pain. He thinks it's just gas colic – you know, like indigestion.'

They were quiet for a little while. It was getting dark and Rhian's face was hidden in shadow, so Mandy couldn't see her expression. Still, it felt peaceful and calm to be sitting there together in the sweet-smelling stable, with only the sound of Camomile's steady breathing to break the silence.

'I'm glad you came over,' Mandy said eventually. 'It sounds like you were a real help.'

'Oh, I didn't do much,' Rhian replied in an offhand voice. She looked up for a second, and her eyes met Mandy's. There was a wary look in them, and Mandy realised immediately that she'd better not try pushing Rhian too far.

'I'm just going to get Camomile over this,' Rhian went on. 'I haven't changed my mind, you know. Don't start thinking I'm going to leap into the saddle and start taking her out every day.'

'No, I won't,' Mandy said hastily. 'I only wanted to say thanks, that's all.'

Then they heard voices outside, and suddenly the stable seemed to be full of people. Rhian's mother was there, clutching a cardigan round her shoulders, with Mrs Tandy and Mandy's dad close behind.

'I thought I'd better come and see how things were going,' Mrs Jones said, looking anxious. 'You've been out here quite a while, Rhian. Maybe it's time you came home for something to eat.'

'I want to stay for a bit longer, Mum,' she replied. 'The vet's only just gone, after all. What if Camomile reacts badly to the medication?'

'She certainly looks comfortable now,' Mr Hope said, watching the mare carefully.

'Oh, she's so much better than she was!' Mrs Tandy exclaimed. 'You should have seen her, pawing with her hind leg as though she wanted to kick her stomach. It was such a relief when Rhian managed to quieten her down.'

'Well, if you're sure, love,' Mrs Jones said, turning to go. 'I'll put your supper in the oven.'

'Speaking of supper,' Mr Hope said, looking at

Mandy, 'I think we should be going home for ours now. Has your mind been set at rest now?'

'Yes, thanks, Dad,' Mandy said, getting stiffly to her feet and rubbing her legs to take away the pins and needles. All things considered, she felt that things hadn't gone too badly at all. Whatever Rhian might say, she couldn't hide the fact that she'd already formed a bond with Camomile. And that bond could only get stronger – Mandy was sure of it.

The four of them started walking back up to the house, leaving Rhian behind in the stable.

'It's so wonderful to see my daughter with a horse again,' Mrs Jones confided to Mandy as they went through the gate and into Mrs Tandy's back garden. 'I've been tearing my hair out, trying to get her riding! Once she's made up her mind about something, she digs in her heels and there's no budging her. Stubborn as a mule, she is.'

'I'm sure she'd enjoy going out on Camomile, if she'd give it a try,' Mandy said.

'It's not only that,' Mrs Jones said, drawing her cardigan more closely round her shoulders. 'Riding does so much for her! All that exercise really helps her muscle tone and obviously being out in the fresh air is good for her too. Rhian hasn't ridden for nearly a year now, and it's breaking my heart to see the state she's in. She hardly goes anywhere these days, and it's getting harder every day for her to walk.' She sighed. 'It's not just the physical side of things, though. She seems so moody most of the time! Sitting up in her bedroom all day is only having a negative effect . . .'

'It must be difficult for her,' Mandy said sympathetically. 'Losing Polo, and then having to move to a strange place.'

'That's another reason I want her to ride!' Mrs Jones said. 'It's such a good way to meet people and make friends.' She took Mandy's arm for a second and looked at her earnestly. 'Nothing I say seems to work – Rhian just does the opposite. If you can think of anything that might persuade her to start riding again, would *you* have a try?'

'Of course,' Mandy said. 'I'll do my best.' But she knew Rhian well enough by now to realise this would be no easy task.

'Thank you so much for coming,' Mrs Tandy said to Mandy and her father, when Mrs Jones had gone home and they were about to leave too. 'I hope I haven't been making too much of a fuss.'

'Not at all,' Mr Hope said. 'You were quite right! Colic can turn very nasty.'

'Besides, at least it brought Camomile and Rhian together,' Mandy added. 'I'm sure you could call on her if you needed any help another time.'

'Well, there's not going to be another time,' Mrs Tandy said firmly. 'I've been thinking things over for a while now, and after what happened today, I've come to a decision. I'm going to sell Camomile – it's the only thing to do.'

Mandy was so shocked she couldn't think what to say for a moment. 'But, Mrs Tandy –' she stammered, 'you can't! You really *can't* sell Camomile now!'

Ten

'I know you've become very fond of Camomile, Mandy,' Mrs Tandy said gently, 'but I'm only trying to do what's best for her. It's not fair to keep her here if I can't look after her properly.'

'You *can* look after her, though,' Mandy said urgently. 'The meadow is perfect, and she's good company for you, and you're taking great care of her!'

'But I can't ride Camomile,' Mrs Tandy said, 'and that's what she needs. The vet told me that her diet is fine, but she needs more exercise or she'll end up getting stressed and colicky again. I can't afford to keep her at livery stables, so finding a good home for her is the only answer. She'll be happier that way.'

'You can see that, can't you, love?' Mr Hope put in, jingling the car keys in his pocket as he stood by the door. 'You've been telling me how much Camomile enjoys her rides with you and James. She needs to be taken out regularly, and if you're honest with yourself, you know you can't manage to do that.'

'Yes, you're right,' Mandy said. 'But there is another alternative.' She turned to Mrs Tandy. 'If there was someone on your doorstep who knew all about horses, someone who could exercise Camomile and help you look after her, would you feel differently?'

'There's no point in speculating, dear,' Mrs Tandy replied. 'There isn't anybody round here like that. I know – I've been making inquiries all week.'

'But there is!' Mandy said excitedly. 'Who managed to calm Camomile down and looked after her until the vet came? Who's sitting with her in the stable now?'

'Rhian?' Mrs Tandy asked doubtfully. 'Well,

she can certainly take care of Camomile. She couldn't possibly ride her, though, could she?'

'Yes, she could!' Mandy exclaimed eagerly, her eyes shining. 'She used to ride all the time, back in Wales! She's just a bit out of practice, that's all.'

'Now come on, Mandy,' her father broke in. 'That's not quite true, is it? You told me Rhian had decided not to ride any more. Remember what I said? You can't force her to change her mind.'

'No, but that was before she'd met Camomile,' Mandy said. 'Things are different now! Besides, her mother's been telling me how much Rhian *needs* to ride. It would help her so much and it would make Camomile happy, too. It's the perfect solution!'

'I don't know, dear,' Mrs Tandy shook her head. 'I couldn't let anyone take Camomile out who couldn't control her properly. What if anything happened? Laura would never forgive me, and I shouldn't think Mrs Jones would be any too pleased either.'

'That's another thing,' Mandy said. 'Have you told Laura you're going to sell Camomile? How does she feel about it?'

Mrs Tandy started to fiddle with the bottom of her cardigan. 'I haven't rung her yet, but I'm going to,' she said, glancing away out of the window. 'She won't be home now, what with the time difference in America. I'll call her just before I go to bed tonight. I know it'll be hard, but she'll have to accept that this is the only answer. She could be in America for years! Camomile is my responsibility now, and I have to decide what's best for her.'

Mandy could tell Mrs Tandy was dreading telling her daughter that Camomile had to be sold. Perhaps she wouldn't mind a reason to put off that phone call for a while. 'Could you wait till the weekend?' she asked. 'James and I can come over on Saturday, and Rhian can try riding Camomile with us then. I know she'll be fine, you'll see!'

'Come on, love, we need to get home,' her father said, opening the front door. 'This isn't your decision, it's up to Mrs Tandy.'

'Please?' Mandy said, pausing for a second on the doorstep as she followed her father out.

'All right,' Mrs Tandy said finally. 'I won't do anything until Saturday. But I should warn you,

Mandy, it'll take a good deal to make me change my mind!'

'Thanks!' Mandy beamed. 'That's great! Oh, and one last thing—'

'Mandy!' her father called from the end of the path. 'Leave Mrs Tandy in peace!'

'Please don't say anything to Rhian about this for the moment,' Mandy went on hurriedly. An idea had begun to form in her mind, though she wasn't sure it could possibly work. 'Thanks again, Mrs Tandy. You won't regret this, I promise!'

For the rest of that week, Mandy rang every day after school to find out how Camomile was doing. Mrs Tandy told her the mare was looking happier every day and, each day, Rhian came to look in on her. On Tuesday, she made Camomile another warm bran mash and held the bucket while she ate it. On Wednesday she spent an hour or so grooming her, and on Thursday, she took her for a walk round the field on a lead rope.

'I haven't said anything to Rhian about selling Camomile,' Mrs Tandy told Mandy when she rang on Friday. 'I really think I should, though. She seems to be getting quite attached to the horse, and I don't want to upset her.'

'Just wait one more day,' Mandy pleaded. 'James and I will be coming tomorrow and you can tell her then, when we're all together. Please, Mrs Tandy!' The idea she'd been mulling over since Monday had turned into a definite plan. She'd talked it over with James, and he felt there was a chance her scheme could work. It had to!

'Well, if you're sure you know what you're doing,' Mrs Tandy replied doubtfully.

'Don't worry, everything will be fine,' Mandy said, trying to convince herself too. 'See you tomorrow – I've got to rush!'

There was no time to talk any longer, because she had to help her parents with the preparations for Sarah's surprise leaving party. Saturday was the student nurse's last day at Animal Ark, but Mrs Hope had discovered she was hurrying away for the weekend as soon as she'd finished morning surgery, so the party would have to be the evening before.

'Sarah's really got the hang of things this week,' Mr Hope said to Mandy as he laid out glasses on the kitchen table. 'She made an excellent job of setting that collie's broken leg. I'll be sorry to see her go.'

'Yes, I will, too,' Mandy said, emptying packets of crisps into a huge pottery bowl. No matter how busy Sarah had been, she'd always found time to have a quick chat with Mandy when she came home after school. And on Tuesday afternoon, Mandy had found a box of chocolate rabbits waiting for her on the kitchen table, with a card from Sarah. *To Mandy and James*, it read, *the best rabbit hunters in Welford!*

'Sarah just needed some time to get used to everything,' Mandy went on, taking a handful of crisps for herself. 'I knew she'd turn out all right in the end.'

Her father tossed a peanut high in the air and caught it neatly in his mouth. 'Yes, your mother was quite right,' he said, after he'd crunched it up. 'As she always is, of course.'

'I heard that, Adam.' Emily Hope smiled, coming through to the kitchen in her white coat. 'And don't think I'm going to let you forget it in a hurry! Now, Mandy, we need your help. Sarah's just finishing up in the surgery. Can you keep her talking for a while, and then find a reason to bring her through here with Jean? That'll give me ten minutes to change and sign her card before everyone else starts arriving.'

'Sure, Mum,' Mandy said, hurrying out of the room. She loved the feeling of excitement in the air before a party began, and the fact that Sarah didn't have a clue what was happening only added to it.

Sarah was polishing some instruments in one of the treatment rooms. 'Hi, there,' Mandy said to her. 'Do you need a hand with that?'

'Oh, it's all right, thanks,' Sarah replied. 'I'm nearly done, and then I'll be off.' She shook her head. 'I still can't quite believe this is my last evening here. These three weeks have gone so quickly!'

'Have you enjoyed yourself?' Mandy asked, picking up a cloth and pitching in.

'Oh, yes!' Sarah replied fervently. 'It's been great. I just wish I'd done a bit better, that's all – not messed up so often. I don't know if I'll ever feel like a proper practice nurse.'

'But you really should!' Mandy protested. 'Think of all the animals you've looked after while you've been here. You've been great, honestly!'

Sarah smiled ruefully, laying down the last pair of tweezers. She was about to speak when, suddenly, Jean burst into the room. 'Sarah – emergency!' she said urgently. 'Coming through!'

A young man was close on her heels, carrying a large tabby cat wrapped up in a towel. He laid this bundle gently on the table and gasped, 'It's Buster. He's pretty bad this time!'

Mandy rushed forward to help Sarah, who was already unwrapping the towel, while Jean took the cat's owner to sit down outside. Buster was desperately struggling to breathe, and anyone could tell he was in serious trouble.

'Have you seen his tongue?' Mandy pointed out quietly to Sarah. It was dark blue.

Sarah nodded. 'Yes, it's an asthma attack – he's not getting enough oxygen,' she replied tersely. 'I'm going to put him in an oxygen tent right away. Mandy, I need you to get your mum or dad and tell them what's happening. And hurry!'

Mandy rushed back into the kitchen. Her father was about to blow a party popper as she hurtled through the door, but he put it down when he saw her face.

'I know Buster,' he said, after Mandy had hurriedly explained what was happening and they were racing through to the surgery. 'He came in last week. Sarah's already giving him oxygen, is she? Good. Let's hope we're in time!'

Sarah looked very relieved when Mr Hope arrived in the treatment room. 'I've put him in the tent with one hundred per cent oxygen,' she said quickly. 'His tongue's beginning to turn pink again. And here's some adrenaline for you.'

'Perfect,' Mr Hope replied, filling a syringe from the bottle. He gave the cat a couple of injections to relax his bronchial muscles and help him breathe. Then he laid down the syringe and wiped his forehead.

'Well done, Sarah,' he said. 'That was a close call. If you hadn't got Buster into the tent so promptly, I don't think he'd have made it. I'll go and tell his owner he's out of danger now. Good job, nurse!'

After he'd gone, Sarah looked at Mandy, her eyes shining. 'Wow! That was amazing!' she said. 'I didn't have time to feel nervous and make a mess of things. And I remembered what to do! Maybe I *am* turning into a real veterinary nurse after all!'

'What have I been telling you?' Mandy said, squeezing her arm. 'You saved Buster's life. It doesn't get more real than that!'

Eleven

The surprise party went perfectly. Sarah had no inkling of what the Hopes had planned and was very touched that so many people had called in to say goodbye and thank her for looking after their pets. Mandy's gran and grandad came too, with a big bunch of flowers from their garden.

'D'you know,' Sarah said to Mandy at the end of the evening, 'I'm in such a good mood I've almost forgotten to feel sad about leaving Animal Ark.'

'Maybe one day you'll come back,' Mandy replied, as she walked with Sarah to the door.

'Keep in touch, won't you? And good luck with your exams!' She was saying goodbye now because her mother was taking her and James over to Mrs Tandy's first thing on Saturday and they probably wouldn't be back until after the end of morning surgery.

Now that all the excitement had died down, Mandy found herself thinking about Camomile and Rhian again. Tomorrow was such an important day: her last chance to keep them together. She'd better not mess it up.

She talked everything over again with James in the car the next morning. 'Your plan's only going to work if Rhian reacts in the way you expect her to,' he said. 'Do you really know her well enough?'

'I think so,' Mandy said, settling back against the car seat. 'I just can't think of any other way of persuading her to ride, can you? This has got to be our only chance.'

They arrived at the bungalow in good time, and Mrs Tandy walked with them down to the meadow. It was great to see Camomile on her feet again. She was waiting by the gate, tossing her head and neighing as they approached.

'Well, you're looking a lot better than the last

time I saw you,' Mandy said. James rubbed the mare's nose as she crunched the peppermint he'd just given her.

Mandy was quiet as she watched Camomile nuzzle James's pocket for more mints. She wondered for one final time whether she was doing the right thing, trying to keep the horse here with Mrs Tandy and Rhian. But she felt sure of the answer – Camomile was well looked after, she had a loving home, and Mandy was convinced that the mare and Rhian could form a very special bond. They were meant for each other.

'Rhian's coming round in a minute,' Mrs Tandy said, as though she could read Mandy's thoughts. 'I'll break the bad news about selling Camomile when she's down here with you. That's what you want, isn't it?'

Mandy nodded. 'But you will let her have a ride if she likes, won't you?' she asked, stroking the mare's satiny neck.

'Only round the field, if you're positive she'll be able to manage,' Mrs Tandy replied. 'I don't think she'll want to, though. She certainly hasn't said anything about it this week, and she's spent plenty of time with Camomile.' She sighed.

'They're getting very close. I hope she's not going to be too upset to think of Camomile leaving.'

Mandy and James were just about to buckle up Camomile's bridle when Rhian and Mrs Tandy let themselves into the field and walked over to the stable. Rhian smiled at Mandy and James, more openly than she'd ever done before, and patted Camomile proudly.

'She's looking good, isn't she?' she said. 'Look at the shine on her coat!'

Mrs Tandy took a deep breath. 'Rhian, there's something I have to tell you,' she began. 'I've mentioned this to Mandy and James already and I ought to let you know, too. I've decided to sell Camomile.'

Rhian looked at Mrs Tandy, startled. Her face turned quite pale, but she didn't say anything. She seemed to be waiting to hear more.

Mrs Tandy put a hand on Camomile's neck, as if to steady herself. 'The thing is, keeping a horse here is too much of a responsibility for me to handle on my own, particularly as I can't ride Camomile myself,' she said. 'I've thought it over carefully, and I'm sure it would be fairer on her if

she went somewhere else. I'm sorry, but that's how I feel.'

'Well, it's your decision,' Rhian said after a pause. 'You have to do what you think is best.'

'Yes, I'm afraid I do,' Mrs Tandy said. She gave Camomile one last pat and then turned to leave. 'Well, have a nice ride, you two. And thanks for everything you've done, Rhian. I'm really grateful for all the help you've given me over the past few days.'

Rhian nodded. When Mrs Tandy was out of earshot, she turned on Mandy and James. 'So you knew about this, did you?' she accused them, with that closed, suspicious look back in her eyes. 'Well, thanks for letting me know.'

'You can't really blame Mrs Tandy,' Mandy shrugged, keeping her voice neutral as she unhooked a stray lock of Camomile's mane from under the bridle's browband. 'Camomile needs exercising, and James and me coming over now and then isn't enough. She's such a great horse to ride. It's terrible to see her going to waste.'

Rhian started to say something, then bit her lip and turned to gaze out over the field. Mandy gave James a meaningful stare.

'Look, don't think we're getting at you, Rhian,' he said, taking the hint. 'No one's expecting you to ride her! You've explained how you feel, and that's fine – we understand.'

Rhian looked at him as though she wasn't quite sure how to respond. 'Anyway,' James went on. 'Look at the size of Camomile! She's not exactly a Shetland, is she? I felt a bit nervous about taking her out the first time I saw her.'

Rhian flushed. 'It's not that—' she began, but Mandy cut her off mid-sentence.

'James, that isn't the point,' she said. 'Rhian's made it perfectly clear she's not interested in riding Camomile. Besides, you know how Mrs Tandy feels. What if Rhian fell off and hurt herself? What would her mother say?'

'So you've discussed this already, have you?' Rhian said, her hands on her hips and colour rising in her cheeks. 'You've been talking about this behind my back and deciding what I should and shouldn't do?'

'No, we haven't,' Mandy said soothingly. 'It was only a crazy idea that came into my head. I thought maybe Mrs Tandy might not sell Camomile if you were willing to ride her, that's all. She wouldn't hear of it, though.'

'And why not, exactly?' Rhian demanded.

'She's only thinking of your safety,' James answered. 'After all, she'd feel responsible if anything happened to you.' He patted the mare's shoulder. 'And, like I said, Camomile might be gentle, but she's a big horse. What if you couldn't control her?'

'No, you helped Camomile get better, and now Mrs Tandy can sell her to someone who'll be able to exercise her,' Mandy added, picking up her hard hat and taking hold of Camomile's reins to lead her off. 'It's for the best.'

'Oh, is it really?' Rhian retorted, two bright spots of colour burning in her cheeks. 'Well, I'm glad you've all had such a cosy time, deciding what's going to happen to Camomile and discussing exactly why I shouldn't ride her! It's OK for you two to take her out but not me – is that it? Because I'd be more likely to fall off, I suppose.'

'We didn't mean it like that!' James said, edging a couple of steps backwards.

'Oh, didn't you?' Rhian said, suddenly taking Mandy's helmet out of her hands and jamming it on her head. 'Well, forgive me for being sensitive, but that's the way it sounds. And now, if you'll be good enough to let me have a turn, I'll take Camomile round the meadow. And I hope Mrs Tandy won't feel that's too dangerous!'

Mandy tried not to let her face betray her feelings as Rhian took Camomile over to the mounting block. They'd succeeded! In the first step, at least. Trying to discourage Rhian from riding Camomile had made her determined to give it a try.

'Well done!' James whispered, as he and Mandy walked a safe distance behind. 'You were dead right about the way she'd react. You know her better than I thought.'

'*I* don't, but her mother does,' Mandy whispered back. 'The other evening, Mrs Jones said to me that if she told Rhian to do something, she always did the opposite. That's what gave me the idea.'

She hurried forward to pull down on the right stirrup while Rhian mounted with the left. It made things easier that Rhian was stronger on the left side, Mandy reflected, as the older girl swung easily into the saddle and bent down to guide her right foot into the stirrup.

'OK?' Mandy asked, looking up. Rhian had calmed down by now, but there was a gleam in her eye that Mandy hadn't seen before. 'Do you want me to lead Camomile for a while?'

'No thanks,' Rhian replied confidently, taking up the reins. 'We'll be fine. I'll start off at a walk until I've got back into the swing of things.'

James and Mandy leaned against the fence and watched as Rhian took Camomile round the field. She held both reins in her left hand, and directed the horse very skilfully with her left leg and rein. Camomile walked beautifully, as graceful and collected as ever, and Rhian sat ramrod straight in the saddle.

'Oh, don't they look good together?' Mandy sighed happily. Rhian glanced over in their direction, her face transformed by a dazzling smile as she urged Camomile into a trot.

'Well?' she called. 'No problem!'

'Great!' Mandy shouted back. 'Let me fetch Mrs Tandy – she'll soon see there's nothing to worry about!'

Mrs Tandy stood by the gate into the field, Mandy and James on either side of her, while Rhian took

Camomile through her paces.

'Don't you think she rides beautifully?' Mandy said persuasively. 'You can tell that she and Camomile are perfectly in tune with each other.'

'And she's taller than we are,' James added. 'Camomile's just the right size for her, whereas she's a little big for us.'

Mrs Tandy smiled. 'I know what you two are up to,' she said. 'Stop trying to twist my arm!'

'But just look how happy Rhian is,' Mandy said. 'I've never seen her like this before. She's loving every minute of it! Couldn't you ask her if she wants to ride Camomile more often?'

'Oh, I don't know,' Mrs Tandy sighed. 'I'm not sure what to do! I was absolutely certain Camomile should be sold after she had that attack of colic, but Rhian's been so good with her this week. And I can't face telling Laura that I want to sell her horse, I must admit. She'd be devastated.'

Rhian and Camomile were cantering now – and then, suddenly, everything began to go wrong. Just after they'd passed by, Rhian started to get into difficulties. She seemed to lose her balance, slipping further and further to one side, and a look of panic came over her face.

'What's happening?' Mandy cried in alarm. If Rhian fell off now, she'd be bound to lose her confidence and all their carefully laid plans would count for nothing. Worse than that, she might seriously hurt herself. Camomile was going at a fast pace.

'She's lost her stirrup!' James said, beginning to climb over the gate. 'The right one.'

Mrs Tandy put her hand on his arm and held him back. 'Let her sort herself out,' she said calmly. 'She'd have to if she was on her own.'

As they watched, Camomile's ears flicked back and she began to change pace – slowing down first to a trot, and then to a walk. Rhian managed to pull herself upright and get her foot back in the stirrup. After a couple of minutes, she was composed again and back in control.

She waved to Mandy and the others to show she was fine, calling, 'I'm still a bit rusty!' before she trotted on again.

'That was amazing!' Mandy exclaimed. 'Camomile realised Rhian was in trouble, so she did what she could to help her.'

'Would you believe it?' Mrs Tandy said.

'Wait till I tell Laura! Well, there's certainly an understanding between those two, and no mistake.'

'Does that mean you'll let Rhian take Camomile out?' Mandy asked, hardly daring to push her luck. 'You can't sell her now, Mrs Tandy, can you? Not after you've seen them together!'

'Well, it all depends what Rhian thinks about exercising Camomile,' Mrs Tandy said. 'She might not want to commit herself. Let's see what she has to say first.'

James waved his arms to attract Rhian and Camomile over to them. 'Are you going to let anyone else have a turn?' he asked, grinning at her after she'd cantered up.

'I'll think about it,' she smiled, swinging her leg over the saddle and holding on to the pommel tightly for a second before lowering herself gently to the ground. 'I'm going to be stiff tomorrow, that's for sure!'

'She's lovely, though, isn't she?' Mandy said, patting Camomile's neck. 'You look great together.'

'Oh, she's wonderful!' Rhian replied, her dark

eyes shining as she gazed at the mare. 'One in a million.'

'Now perhaps we should have a talk,' Mrs Tandy said seriously, laying her hand on Rhian's arm. 'You know what I said before, about selling Camomile? Well, I can see how much you've enjoyed riding her and what a good pair you make. That does change things.'

Rhian looked at Mrs Tandy, her eyes wide, as though she had half an idea what might be coming next but hardly dared to hope it could be true.

'I know already that you can help me take care of Camomile,' Mrs Tandy went on. 'If you were able to exercise her too, we could try keeping her here – at least for a trial period. But it's up to you, dear. It's a big commitment and I'm not going to put any pressure on you to decide.'

Mandy held her breath. How would Rhian respond? What if she was still not prepared to get involved? She must know by now just how special Camomile was – surely she couldn't turn down the chance to ride her as often as she wanted?

Rhian stroked Camomile's smooth nose for a moment without speaking. 'She's a beautiful horse,' she said eventually. 'I didn't want to get too close to her, but I couldn't help it in the end. And I'm glad things have turned out this way. If you do have to sell Camomile then I'll accept it, though I won't ever forget her. But if you keep her, then I'll ride her, and look after her, and love her as if she was my very own. That's a promise!'

Mandy felt as though she was going to explode. Yes! This was more than she could have hoped for! 'Oh, Mrs Tandy!' she said, almost bursting with excitement. 'You won't sell Camomile now, will you? You couldn't!'

'No, I don't suppose I could,' Mrs Tandy laughed. 'All right! We'll keep her here in the meadow for the moment and see how things go.'

Rhian was lost for words, but she didn't need to say anything to show how she was feeling. The look of joy on her face was clear to see. She laid her head against Camomile's smooth neck for a second, while the mare nuzzled her hair gently.

Mandy threw out her arms and gave Mrs Tandy a big hug. She'd have done the same to James and Rhian too, but they both dodged away, laughing, so she hugged Camomile tightly instead. She was certain that things were going to go very well indeed!

Another Hodder Children's book

CATS IN THE CARAVAN

Lucy Daniels

Mandy and James discover a feral cat and her kittens behind old Wilfred Bennet's cottage. But the next time they visit, she's moved her family into a caravan on Sam Western's campsite! Can Mandy and James tempt the cats out before Mr Western causes trouble?

PORPOISE IN THE POOL
Animal Ark Summer Special

Lucy Daniels

Mandy and James are spending their summer holiday at Sennen Cove in Cornwall. The cove is very popular with young jetskiers, but Mandy is worried they will disturb the nearby school of harbour porpoises. Her fears are realised when she and James find an injured porpoise trapped in a rock pool. Can Mandy and James help nurse the frightened creature back to health – and persuade the jetskiers to stop endangering the porpoises?